The Vineyards of Calanetti
Saying "I do" under the Tuscan sun...

Deep in the Tuscan countryside nestles
the picturesque village of Monte Calanetti.
Famed for its world-renowned vineyards, the
village is also home to the crumbling but beautiful
Palazzo di Comparino. Empty for months, rumors of
a new owner are spreading like wildfire...and that's
before the village is chosen as the setting for the
royal wedding of the year!

It's going to be a roller coaster of a year, but will
wedding bells ring out in Monte Calanetti for
anyone else?

Find out in this fabulously heartwarming, uplifting
and thrillingly romantic new eight-book continuity
from Harlequin Romance!

A Bride for the Italian Boss by Susan Meier

Return of the Italian Tycoon by Jennifer Faye

Reunited by a Baby Secret by Michelle Douglas

Soldier, Hero...Husband? by Cara Colter

His Lost-and-Found Bride by Scarlet Wilson
Available September 2015

The Best Man & the Wedding Planner
by Teresa Carpenter

His Princess of Convenience by Rebecca Winters

Saved by the CEO by Barbara Wallace

Dear Reader,

As a writer, it is always fun to be invited to write on a continuity series. I appreciate how much hard work happens behind the scenes as editors begin to put together a concept, a setting and a framework. All this work makes its way into a "bible," which outlines the setting, the characters and the stories within the series.

The bible is sent to each of the writers who have been selected to work on this series. And then the emails, ideas, pictures, maps and clarifications fly back and forth between us. I have not counted them, but I am willing to bet I have in the neighborhood of two hundred emails concerning this set of stories that take place in the gorgeous sun-drenched vineyards of Tuscany.

It is a truly amazing thing to be in the flow of such an abundance of creative energy. Writing can be a lonely business, and so it's a nice change to be connected with fellow writers for a little while. I hope you, the reader, can feel the magic that happens when a team of women unites to make the world a tiny bit better with their messages of hope and love. I know I did.

With warmest wishes,

Cara Colter

Soldier, Hero...
Husband?

—

Cara Colter

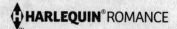

Recycling programs for this product may not exist in your area.

Special thanks and acknowledgment are given to Cara Colter for her contribution to The Vineyards of Calanetti series.

ISBN-13: 978-0-373-74356-8

Soldier, Hero...Husband?

First North American Publication 2015

Copyright © 2015 by Harlequin Books S.A.

HARLEQUIN®
™ www.Harlequin.com

Printed in U.S.A.

Cara Colter shares her life in beautiful British Columbia, Canada, with her husband, nine horses and one small Pomeranian with a large attitude. She loves to hear from readers, and you can learn more about her and contact her through Facebook.

Books by Cara Colter

HARLEQUIN ROMANCE

Mothers in a Million

Second Chance with the Rebel

The Gingerbread Girls

Snowflakes and Silver Linings

The Cop, the Puppy and Me
Battle for the Soldier's Heart
How to Melt a Frozen Heart
Rescued by the Millionaire
The Millionaire's Homecoming
Interview with a Tycoon
Meet Me Under the Mistletoe
The Pregnancy Secret

Visit the Author Profile page
at Harlequin.com for more titles.

To the team of editors and writers who worked so tirelessly on this series:

I am proud to have been a part of it.

I stand in awe of your creative brilliance.

CHAPTER ONE

CONNOR BENSON AWOKE with a start. It was dark. And it was hot. Where was he? Somalia? Iraq? Afghanistan? Wherever he was, it was so secret, even his mother didn't know.

That feeling tickled along his spine, a sense of imminent danger. It brought him to red alert. Still not knowing exactly where he was, he was suddenly extremely focused, on nothing and everything. Each of his senses was so wide-open it was almost painful.

The tick of a clock somewhere in the room seemed explosively loud. Connor could feel the faint prickliness of the bedclothes against his naked skin, and he could feel a single bead of sweat slide down his temple. He could smell the residue of his own sweat and aftershave, and farther away, coffee.

Another sound rose above the ticking of the clock and the deliberate steadiness of his own breathing. It was a whispery noise just beyond this room, and as unobtrusive as it was, Connor knew it was that sound that had woken him. It was the sneaky sound of someone trying to be very quiet.

Connor tossed off the thin blanket and was out of the bed in one smooth movement, from dead asleep to warrior alert in the time it took to draw a single breath. The floor was stone under his bare feet and he moved across it soundlessly. His nickname on his SEAL team had been "the Cat."

At six foot five, every inch of that honed muscle, his comrades didn't mean a friendly house cat, either.

They meant the kind of cat that lived like a shadow on the edge of the mountains, or in the deepest forests and the darkest jungles, where men were afraid to go. They meant the kind of cat that was big and strong and silent. They meant the kind of cat that could go from relaxed to ready to pounce in the blink of an eye. They meant the kind of cat that had deadly and killing instincts.

Those instincts guided Connor across the room on silent feet to the door that had a faint sliver of light slipping under it. His movement was seemingly unhurried, but his muscles were tensing with lethal purpose.

Though most people would have detected no scent at all, when he paused on his side of the door, just under the aroma of coffee, Connor could taste the air. He *knew* someone was on the other side of that door. He also knew they were not directly in front of it—a hint of a shadow told him someone was to the left of the door. It was not a guess. His muscles tautened even more. His heart began to pick up the tempo. Not with fear. No, there was no fear at all. What he felt was anticipation.

Adrenaline coursed through his veins as Connor flung open the door.

He was nearly blinded by sunlight in the hallway, but it didn't stop his momentum. He hurled himself left, at the figure, back to him, rising from a crouch beside his door well. His hands closed around slender shoulders.

Slender?

A scent he had not noticed before tickled his nostrils.

Perfume?

His mind screamed, *Abort!* It was too late not to touch, but not too late to temper his considerable strength. Instead of taking the culprit to the ground, he used the existing momentum to spin the person skulking outside his door toward him. The force of the spin caused a stumble, and as luscious curves came in full contact with him, Connor recognized the truth.

Her.

Connor stared down into the eyes of the woman he had just attacked, stunned. It wasn't that women couldn't be bad guys, but this woman so obviously was not. He cursed under his breath, and her eyes, already wide, widened more.

She seemed to realize she was still pressed, full length, against him, and she pushed herself away.

"Ma sei pazzo!" she said. Her voice was gorgeous, husky and rich, a note of astonishment in it that matched the astonishment in her huge, wide eyes. She definitely had the most beautiful eyes he had ever seen.

Eyes that, at the moment, were wide with shock. Now that she had pushed away from him, her hand went to the sweet swell of her breast, and he could see where her pulse beat wildly in the delicate column of her throat.

Connor, ever the soldier, and still in that place of heightened awareness, took in every exquisite detail of her. She had long, dark hair, luxuriously thick and straight, that was capturing the incredible morning light that poured in through the arched windows of the hallway they were in. Her hair fell in a shimmering waterfall of dark chocolate past slender bare shoulders.

At least a foot shorter than he was, the woman had on a bright, flower-patterned dress. It was sleeveless and accentuated the lovely litheness of her figure. The dress was pinched by a narrow belt at a tiny waist and then the skirt flared out in a way that made him able to picture her dancing, that skirt flying around her. She had sandals on her delicate feet, her toenails painted a soft shade of pink.

Her coloring looked as if it was naturally pale, but golden from the sun. Her skin was flawless. *Ma sei pazzo.* It occurred to Connor he was not in Iraq. Or Somalia. Not Afghanistan, either.

He cringed inwardly at his mistake. "Jeez," he said, out loud. "I'm in Italy."

It all came back to him. He was in a small town in Tuscany on a puffball mission for Itus Security, the company he and his friend Justin had started after Justin's injury had made them both leave the US Navy SEALs, though for different reasons.

"Sì, Italia."

Yes, he was in Italy. And it was not a secret. Everyone in his world, including his mother, knew exactly where he was. In fact, his mother had been thrilled for him when he had told her the Tuscan village of Monte Calanetti was on his itinerary.

Italy? she had said breathlessly. She had looked at him with ridiculously hope-filled eyes and said softly, *The land of amore.*

If anybody had a right to be soured by love, it was his mom, who'd had him when she was barely sixteen and had suffered through all it meant to be a single mother at that age.

In addition, Connor knew exactly what his years of service in the world's trouble spots and danger zones had made him. He knew only a mother could look at a battle-hardened and emotionally bereft specimen like Connor and hope love was in his future.

"Do you speak English?" he asked the young woman. He kept his voice deliberately quiet, threading it with calm. The woman was still watching him silently, with those doe-like eyes, and just like a doe, was ready to bolt at one more wrong move from him.

She nodded warily.

He deserved her wariness. "Sorry, ma'am," he muttered. "I seem to have a bit of jet lag. I was disoriented."

"You came out of that room as if you expected an assassin!" she said accusingly, finding her voice.

No point sharing with her that was exactly what he had been expecting. There was something sweetly angelic in her face that suggested that would be entirely foreign to her world.

Looking at her, it did occur to Connor that if a man was not completely hardened to life, the woman in front of him—beautiful and angelic, yet still sensual in an understated way—might have made his thoughts go to *amore*.

"I said I was sorry. I hope I didn't hurt you." Connor had tempered his strength, but even so, she was right. He had come out of that room expecting trouble of one variety or another, and his force had been substantial.

"No. No, I'm not hurt," she insisted hastily, but then she folded her hands over her shoulders and rubbed them.

He stepped in close to her again, aware of her scent intensifying. He carefully pried her hands off her shoulders. She stopped breathing, staring up at him, her hands drifting to her sides.

If he was not mistaken, he stopped breathing, too, as he leaned in close and inspected the golden surface of her shoulders for damage. He stepped back and started to breathe again.

"There are no marks on your shoulders," he said quietly. "You won't be bruised."

"I told you I was fine."

He shrugged, looked away from her, ran a hand through his hair and then looked back. "I just thought I should make sure. What does that mean? What you said to me? *Ma sei pazzo?*"

"It's an exclamation of surprise," she said.

It was her eyes sliding away from him that alerted him to the fact there might be more to it than that, so he lifted an eyebrow at her, waiting.

"Specifically," she said, looking back at him, "it means *are you crazy?*" She was unrepentant, tilting her chin at him.

"Ah. Well. I can't really argue with that, or blame you for thinking it."

His senses were beginning to stand down, but even so, the woman's scent tickled his nostrils. Her perfume was very distinctive—

it had an exotic, spicy scent that was headier than any perfume he had ever smelled. He looked once more into the liquid pools of green and gold that were her eyes and recognized a weak inclination to fall toward those pools of light and grace, calm and decency.

Instead, he reminded himself who he really was. He let his thoughts travel away from her and down the road to the sense of failure that traveled with him these days, around the globe, like a shadow.

What had just happened was precisely why he'd had to leave the only world he had known for nearly two decades. He'd started making mistakes. It was why he had left the SEALs when Justin had. In his line of work, mistakes demanded a price be paid. Often it was a huge price. Sometimes it was an irrevocable one.

And he knew, from firsthand experience, it was even harder when it was someone other than yourself who paid the price for your mistakes.

"It's all right," she stammered, and he realized she had seen something in his face that he would have preferred she hadn't seen.

And of course it was not all right to be attacking innocent civilians. Now that the initial shock had worn off, Connor could see she was trembling slightly, like a leaf in a breeze, and her eyes were wide on him. Her gaze flitted down the length of him, and then flew back to his face, shocked.

He glanced down at himself.

"Sheesh," he muttered. "Would that be adding insult to injury?"

"I told you I wasn't injured," she stammered. "And I'm not sure what you mean by insulted."

"It's an expression," he clarified, "just like your *ma sei pazzo*. It means on top of giving you a good scare, I've embarrassed you with my state of undress."

Her eyes flew to his state of undress, again, and then back up to his face. She confirmed that she was indeed embarrassed when her blush deepened to crimson.

He would probably be blushing himself if he had any scrap of modesty remaining in himself, but he did not. He'd lived in the rough company of men his entire adult life and guys had a tendency to be very comfortable in their underwear.

Still, he was very aware that he was standing in this beautiful woman's presence outfitted only in army-green boxer briefs that covered only the essential parts of himself.

Despite the circumstances he found himself in, he was reluctantly charmed that she was blushing so profusely it looked as if she had been standing with her face too close to a robust fire.

"Sorry, I'm disoriented," he said again, by way of explanation. "I've been on an insane schedule. I was in—" he had to think about it for a second "—Azerbaijan yesterday putting a security team in place for the World Food Conference. And the day before that… ah, never mind."

She struggled to regain her composure. "You're Signor Benson, of course."

"Connor, please."

"I'm sorry I was not here to greet you last night. Nico told me you would arrive late." Her English, he noted, was perfect, the accent lilting and lovely in the background of the precisely formed words. Her voice itself was enchanting, husky and unconsciously sensual. Or maybe it was that accent that just made everything she said seem insanely pleasing. Connor was willing to bet she could read a grocery list and sound sexy. He felt, crazily, as if he could listen to her all day.

"I think it was close to three in the morning when I arrived."

She nodded. "Nico told me your arrival would be very late. That's why I closed the shutters when I prepared your room. To block out the light so you could sleep in. I was just leaving you something to eat this morning. I have to be at work in a few minutes."

"Schoolteacher?" he guessed.

She frowned at him. "Nico told you that?"

"No, I guessed."

"But how?"

"You just have that look about you."

"Is this a good thing or a bad thing to have this look about me?"

He shrugged, realizing he shouldn't have said anything. It was part of what he did. He was very, very good at reading people. He could almost always tell, within seconds, what kind of lifestyle someone had, the general direction of their career paths and pursuits, if not the specifics. Sometimes his life and the lives of others depended on that ability to accurately read and sort details. This was something she, living here in her sheltered little village in Italy, did not have to know.

"I still do not understand if it is a good thing or a bad thing to have this schoolteacher look about me," she pressed.

"A good thing," he assured her.

She looked skeptical.

"You're very tidy. And organized." He gestured at the tray beside his door. "And thoughtful, closing the shutters so I could sleep in. So, I figured some profession that required compassion. A teacher. Or a nurse. But the dress made me lean toward teacher. Your students probably like bright colors."

He was talking *way* too much, which he put down as another aftereffect of jet lag. She was nibbling her lip, which was plump as a plum, and frowning at him.

"It's like a magician's trick," she said, not approvingly.

"No, really, it's something everyone can do. It's just observing details."

She looked as if she was considering having another long, hard look at all of him, as if he had invited her to play a parlor game. But then, wisely, she decided against it.

Connor glanced at the tray set so carefully by his door, more proof of a tidy, organized, caring personality. It was loaded with a carafe of coffee and rolls still steaming from the oven. There was a small glass jar of homemade preserves and a large orange.

The fact he had guessed right about her

being a teacher did not alleviate his annoyance with himself over this other stupid error. He'd heard someone sneaking around, all right—sneaking his breakfast into place so as not to disturb him.

"Thank you," he said, "for taking me in on such short notice. I should have made arrangements for a place to stay before I arrived, but I didn't think it was going to be a problem. When I researched it, there seemed to be lots of accommodations in the village."

"There are many accommodations here, and usually there would be more availability," she offered. "Today looks as if it will be an exception, but it is usually not overly hot in May. That makes it the preferred month for weddings in Tuscany."

Weddings.

"Ah, signor," she said, and the fright had finally melted from her and a tiny bit of playfulness twinkled in her eyes. "You are right! Sometimes you can see things about people that they don't tell you."

"Such as?"

"Even though you are here to help with the royal wedding, you do not like weddings."

What he didn't like was being read as easily as he read other people. Had he actually encouraged this observation? He hoped not.

"What makes you say that?" he asked.

"Just a little flinch," she said, and for a moment he thought she was going to reach over and touch his face, but she thought better of it and touched the line of her own jaw instead. "Right here."

Her fright had brought out his protective instincts, even though he had caused it. Her power of observation, brought out with just the tiniest of suggestions, was somehow far more dangerous to him. He noticed she had ignored his invitation to call him by his first name.

"I'm not exactly here to help with the wedding," he said, just in case she had the absurd notion he was going to be arranging flowers or something. "My company, Itus, will be providing the security. I'm going to do reconnaissance this month so all the pieces will be in place for when we come back at the end of July. Though you are right on one count—weddings are just about my least favorite thing," he admitted gruffly.

"You've experienced many?" She raised an eyebrow at him, and again he felt danger in the air. Was she teasing him, ever so slightly?

"Unfortunately, I have experienced many weddings," Connor said.

"Unfortunately?" she prodded. "Most people would see a wedding as a celebration of all that is good in life. Love. Hope. Happy endings."

"Humph," he said, not trying to hide his cynicism. Over his years in the SEALs, lots of his team members had gotten married. And with predictably disastrous results. The job was too hard on the women who were left behind to fret and worry about their husbands. Or worse, who grew too lonely and sought someone else's company.

He was not about to share his personal revelations about the fickle nature of love with her, though. Around a woman like her—who saw weddings as symbols of love and hope and happy endings—it was important to reveal nothing personal, to keep everything on a professional level.

"My company, Itus Security," Connor said, veering deliberately away from his personal experiences, "has handled security for some very high-profile nuptials. As a security detail, weddings are a nightmare. Too many variables. Locations. Guests. Rehearsals. Photos. Dinners. And that's before you factor in Bridezilla and her entourage."

"Bridezilla?" she asked, baffled.

Some things did not translate. "Bride turned monster over her big day."

His hostess drew in a sharp breath. "I do not think you will find Christina Rose like that," she said sternly. "She is an amazing woman who is sweet and generous and totally committed to her country."

Connor cocked his head at her. He was hopeful for any inside information that might prove useful to the security detail. "You know her?"

She looked embarrassed all over again, but this time there was annoyance in it, too. "Of course not. But her husband-to-be, Prince Antonio de l'Accardi, is a member of a much-loved royal family. That has made her a very famous woman. I have read about her."

"Well, don't believe half of what you read. No, don't believe *any* of what you read."

"So, you don't believe in weddings, and you are a cynic, also."

"Cynic is an understatement. I think you might have picked up I was a bit of a battle-hardened warrior when I treated you like an assassin instead of just saying good morning like a normal person would have," he said.

There. Letting her know, right off the bat, he was not a normal person.

"Well, I choose to believe Christina Rose is everything she appears to be." Her eyes rested on him, and he heard, without her saying a word, *And so are you.*

Connor lifted a shoulder, noting that his hostess had a bit of fire underneath that angelic first impression. It didn't matter to him what the future princess's personality was. It would be her big day, laden with that thing he was most allergic to, emotion. And it didn't matter to him what his hostess's personality was, either.

"Believe me," he muttered, "Christina Rose will find a million ways, intentional or not, to make my life very difficult."

But that was why he was here, nearly two months early, in the Tuscan village of Monte Calanetti. Not to save the world from bad guys, but to do risk assessment, to protect some royals he had never heard of from a country he had also never heard of—Halenica—as they exchanged their vows.

That was his mission. The lady in front of him could fill his life with complications, too, if he was not the disciplined ex-soldier that he was. As it was, he was not going to be sidetracked by a little schoolteacher in a flowered dress, no matter how cute she was.

And she was plenty cute.

But if that proved a problem, he would just keep his ear to the ground for another place to stay. He'd survived some pretty rough living arrangements. He wasn't fussy.

"Thank you for breakfast," he said curtly, moving into emotional lockdown, work mode. "Please thank your mother for providing me with a place to stay on such short notice, signorina."

"My mother?"

"Signora Rossi?"

A tiny smile, pained, played across the beautiful fullness of her lips.

"No, signor. I am Signora Rossi. Please call me Isabella."

So he had made another mistake. A small one, but a mistake, nonetheless. Looking at Isabella, after she made that statement, he could see, despite his finely honed powers of observation, he'd been wrong about her. She was not as young as her slender figure and flawless skin had led him to believe. She might have been in her thirties, not her twenties.

No wonder Justin had him on wedding duty. Connor was just making mistakes all over the place.

And no wonder Justin had said to Connor, when he gave him this assignment, "Hey, when is the last time you had a holiday? Take your time in Monte Calanetti. Enjoy the sights. Soak up some sun. Drink some wine. Fall in love."

Justin really had no more right to believe in love than he himself did, but his friend was as bad as his mother in the optimism department. Justin had even hinted there was a woman friend in his life.

"And for goodness' sake," Justin had said, "take a break from swimming. *What* are you training for, anyway?"

But Justin, his best friend, his comrade in arms, his brother, was part of the reason Connor swam. Justin, whose whole life had been changed forever because of a mistake. One made by Connor.

So giving up swimming was out of the question, but at least, Connor told himself grimly, he wouldn't be falling in love with the woman in front of him. After having felt her pressed against him, and after having been so aware of her in every way this morning, it was a relief to find out she was married.

"*Grazie*, Signora Rossi," he said, trying out clumsy Italian, "for providing me with accommodation on such short notice. You can reassure your husband that I will not begin every morning by attacking you."

His attempt at humor seemed to fall as flat as his Italian. He spoke three languages well, and several more not so well. Connor knew, from his international travels, that most people warmed to someone who attempted to use their language, no matter how clumsy the effort.

But his hostess looked faintly distressed.

And then he realized he had made his worst mistake of the day, and it wasn't that he had accidentally propositioned her by mispronouncing a word.

Because Isabella Rossi said to him, with quiet dignity, "I'm afraid my beloved husband, Giorgio, is gone, signor. I am a widow."

Connor wanted to tell her that she of all people, then, should not believe a wedding was a symbol of love and hope and happy endings.

But he considered himself a man who was something of an expert in the nature of courage, and he had to admit he reluctantly admired her ability to believe in hope and happy endings when, just like his mother, she had obviously had plenty of evidence to the contrary.

"I'm sorry for your loss," he offered, grudgingly.

"My husband has been gone six years, and I miss him still," she said softly.

Connor felt the funniest stir of something he did not like. Was it envy? Did he envy the man this woman had loved so deeply?

Stupid jet lag. It seemed to have opened up a part of him that normally would have been under close guard, buttoned down tight. Thoroughly annoyed with himself and his wayward thoughts in the land of *amore*, Connor turned from Signora Isabella Rossi, scooped up the tray and went into his room. Just before he shut the door, her voice stopped him.

"I provide a simple dinner at around seven for my guests, when I have them," she said, suddenly all business. "If you could let me know in the mornings if you are requiring this service, I would appreciate it."

Connor, a man who was nothing if not deeply instinctual, knew there was some dangerous physical awareness between them, a primal man-woman thing. Eating her food and sitting across a table from her would not be an option.

On the other hand, he did not know the lay of the land in the village, and he would have to eat somewhere today until he figured that out. Besides, Isabella Rossi had shown she was unusually astute at reading people. He did not want her to know he perceived her as such a threat that he was willing to go hungry rather than spend more time with her.

"Thank you," he said, keeping his tone carefully neutral. "That would be perfect for tonight. I hope the rest of your day goes better than it began, signora."

CHAPTER TWO

ISABELLA STOOD IN the hallway, feeling frozen to the spot and looking at Connor Benson, balancing the tray of food she had provided for him on the jutting bone of one very sexy, very exposed hip. She felt as if she had been run over by a truck.

Which, in a sense, she had. Not that Connor Benson looked anything like a truck. But she had been virtually run down by him, had felt the full naked strength of him pressed against her own body. It had been a disconcerting encounter in every way.

His scent was still tickling her nostrils, and she was taken aback by how much she liked the exquisitely tangy smell of a man in the morning.

Now she'd gone and offered him dinner. Everyone in town knew she occasionally would take in a lodger for a little extra money.

She always offered her guests dinner. Why was it suddenly a big deal?

It was because her guests were usually retired college professors or young travelers on a budget. She not had a guest quite like Connor Benson before. In fact, it would be quite safe to say she had never met a man like Connor Benson before.

"I hope my day goes better, too," she muttered, and then added in Italian, "but it is not looking hopeful."

This man in her house, who stood before her unself-conscious in his near nakedness, was the antithesis of everything Isabella's husband, Giorgio, had been.

In fact, Isabella had grown up in Florence and walked nearly daily by the Palazzo Vecchio, where the replica of Michelangelo's statue *David* stood. The statue represented a perfection of male physique that had filled the frail Giorgio with envy, and at which she had scoffed.

"Such men do not exist," she had reassured Giorgio. She had swept her hand over the square. "Look. Show me one who looks like this."

And then they would dissolve into giggles

at the fact the modern Italian male was quite far removed from Michelangelo's vision.

And yet this nearly naked man standing in the doorway of the room she had let to him made Isabella uncomfortably aware that not only did perfection of male physique exist, it awakened something in her that she had never quite felt before.

That thought made her feel intensely guilty, as if she was being disloyal to her deceased husband, and so she rationalized the way she was feeling.

It was because she had been pulled so unexpectedly against the hard length of him that her awareness was so intense, she told herself.

Her defenses had been completely down. She had just been innocently putting his breakfast beside his door when he had catapulted out of it and turned her around, making her stumble into him.

And now her whole world felt turned around, because she had endured a forced encounter with the heated silk of his skin, stretched taut over those sleek muscles. She had been without the company of a man for a long time. This kind of reaction to a complete stranger did not reflect in any way on her relationship with Giorgio! It was the absence of male companionship that had obviously made her very sensitive to physical contact.

It didn't help that Connor Benson was unbelievably, sinfully gorgeous. Not just the perfection of his male form, but his face was extraordinary. His very short cropped light brown hair only accentuated the fact that he had a face that would make people—especially women people—stop in their tracks.

He had deep blue eyes, a straight nose, high cheekbones, a jutting chin.

He was the epitome of strength. She thought of his warrior response to her outside his door, that terrifying moment when she had been spun around toward him, the look on his face, as if it was all *normal* for him.

There was something exquisitely dangerous about Connor Benson.

The thoughts appalled her. They felt like a betrayal of Giorgio, whom she had loved, yes, with all her heart.

"I've become pathetic," Isabella muttered to herself, again in Italian. A pathetic young widow, whose whole life had become her comfy house and the children she taught. She found love in the mutual adoration she and her students had for each other.

Why did it grate on her that her houseguest

had known she was a schoolteacher? What would she have wanted him to think she was?

Something, she realized reluctantly, just a little more exciting.

"I'm sorry?" Connor said.

She realized she had mumbled about her self-diagnosis of being pathetic out loud, though thankfully, in Italian. She realized her face was burning as if the inner hunger he had made her feel was evident to him.

Well, it probably was. Men like this—powerfully built, extraordinarily handsome, oozing self-confidence—were used to using their looks to charm women, to having their wicked way. They were not above using their amazing physical charisma to make conquests.

He'd already told her how he felt about weddings, which translated to an aversion to commitment. Even she, for all that she had married young and lived a sheltered life, knew that a man like this one standing before her, so at ease with near nakedness, spelled trouble, in English or Italian, and all in capital letters, too.

This man could never be sweetly loyal and uncomplicated. Connor Benson had warned her. He was not normal. He was cynical and hard and jaded. She could see that in the deep blue of his eyes, even if he had not admitted it to her, which he had. She would have been able to see it, even before he had challenged her to look for details to know things about people that they were not saying.

"I said be careful of the shower," she blurted out.

That exquisite eyebrow was raised at her, as if she had said something suggestive.

"It isn't working properly," she said in a rush.

"Oh?"

"I'm having it fixed, but the town's only plumber is busy with the renovations at the palazzo. I have to wait for him. Now, I'm late for work," she choked out, looking at her wristwatch to confirm that. Her wrist was naked—she had not put on her watch this morning. She stared at the blank place on her wrist a moment too long, then hazarded another look at Mr. Benson.

The sensuous line of Connor Benson's mouth lifted faintly upward. The hunger that unfurled in her belly made her think of a tiger who had spotted raw meat after being on a steady diet of flower petals.

Isabella turned and fled.

And if she was not mistaken, the soft notes of a faintly wicked chuckle followed her before Connor Benson shut his bedroom door.

Outside her house, Isabella noted the day was showing promise of unusual heat. She told herself that was what was making her face feel as if it was on fire as she hurried along the twisted, cobbled streets of Monte Calanetti to the primary school where she taught.

Yes, it was the heat, not the memory of his slow drawl, the way *ma'am* had slipped off his lips. He sounded like one of the cowboys in those old American Western movies Giorgio had enjoyed so much when he was bedridden.

Really? The way Connor Benson said *ma'am* should have been faintly comical. How come it was anything but? How come his deep voice and his slow drawl had been as soft as a silk handkerchief being trailed with deliberate seduction over the curve of her neck?

She thought of Connor Benson's attempt at Italian when he had tried to assure that her mornings would not begin with an attack. That accent should have made that comical, too, but it hadn't been. She had loved it that he had tried to speak her language.

"*Buongiorno*, Signora Rossi. You look beautiful this morning!"

Isabella smiled at the butcher, who had come out of his shop to unwind his awning, but once she was by him, she frowned. She passed him every morning. He always said good morning. But he had never added that she looked beautiful before.

It was embarrassing. Her encounter with Connor Benson this morning had lasted maybe five minutes. How was it that it had made her feel so uncomfortable, so hungry and so alive? And so much so that she was radiating it for others to see?

"Isabella," she told herself sternly, using her best schoolteacher voice, "that is quite enough."

But it was not, apparently, quite enough.

Because she found herself thinking that she had not told him anything about his accommodations. She could do that over dinner tonight.

Isabella was *never* distracted when she was teaching. She loved her job and her students and always felt totally present and engaged when she was with the children. Her job, really, was what had brought her back from the brink of despair after Giorgio's death.

But today, her mind wandered excessively to what kind of meal she would cook for her guest.

Candles, of course, would be ridiculous, wouldn't they? And they would give the wrong message entirely.

She had not made her mother's recipe of *lasagne verdi al forno* for years. Food, and finally even the smell of cooking, had made Giorgio sick. Isabella was shocked at how much she *wanted* to cook, to prepare a beautiful meal. Yes, lasagna, and a fresh loaf of ciabatta bread, a lovely red wine. School in many places in Italy, including Monte Calanetti, ran for six days instead of five, but the days were short, her workday over at one. That gave her plenty of time to cook the extravagant meal.

So, on the way home from school, she stopped at the grocer's and the bakery and picked up everything she needed. She had several beautiful bottles of wine from Nico's Calanetti vineyard that she had never opened. Wine opened was meant to be drunk. It had seemed silly and wasteful to open a whole bottle for herself.

From the deep silence in the house, Isabella knew that Connor was not there when she arrived home. Already, it occurred to her she knew his scent, and her nose sniffed the air for him.

She began unloading the contents of her grocery bags in her homey little kitchen. She considered putting on a fresh dress. One that would make him rethink his assessment of her as a schoolteacher. It was then that Isabella became aware that it wasn't just the idea of cooking that was filling her with this lovely sense of purpose.

It was the idea of cooking for a man.

She stopped what she was doing and sat down heavily at her kitchen table.

"Isabella," she chided herself, "you are acting as if this is a date. It's very dangerous. You are out of your league. You will only get hurt if you play games with a man like Connor Benson."

She was also aware she felt faintly guilty, as if this intense awareness of another man—okay, she would call a spade a spade, she was attracted to Connor Benson—was a betrayal of the love she had had with Giorgio.

Everyone kept telling her it was time to move on, and in her head she knew they were right. Six years was a long time for a woman to be alone. If she did not make a move soon, she would probably never have the children she longed for.

But no matter what her head said, her heart said no. Her heart had been hurt enough for this lifetime. Her heart did not want to fall in love ever again.

Slowly, feeling unreasonably dejected, she put everything away instead of leaving it out to cook with. She would bring anything that would spoil to school tomorrow and give it to Luigi Caravetti. He was from a single-parent family, and she knew his mother was struggling right now.

She opened a can of soup, as she would have normally done, and broke the bread into pieces. She would invite Connor to share this humble fare with her when he arrived. She needed to go over things with him, make clear what she did and did not provide.

It wasn't very much later that he came in the front door. She felt she was ready. Or as ready as a woman could ever be for a man like that.

"I have soup if you would like some," she called out formally.

"*Grazie*, that sounds great."

Isabella wished Connor would not try to speak Italian. It made her not want to be formal at all. It made her long to teach him a few words or phrases, to correct his pronunciation. She listened as he went up the stairs. She heard the shower turn on. Her mind went to the memory of touching that perfect body this morning, and something shivered along her spine. It was a warning. If she was smart there would be no language lessons with Connor Benson.

A little while later, he came into the kitchen. Oh, God. He was so big in this tiny room. It was as if he took up all the space. Her eyes felt as if they wanted to go anywhere but to him.

But where else could they go, when he was taking up all the space?

He was freshly showered. He had on a clean shirt. He smelled wonderful. His hair was dark and damp, and towel roughened. He had not shaved, so his whiskers were thick, and she could almost imagine how they would feel scraping across a woman's skin.

"I hope you don't expect homemade," she said. Her voice sounded like a croak.

"I didn't expect anything at all, ma'am."

There was that *ma'am* again, slow and steady, dragging across the back of her neck, drugging her senses.

"Isabella." Her voice sounded like a whisper. "Please, sit."

He took a seat at her table. It made her table seem ridiculous, as if it had been made to go in a dollhouse.

"Isabella," he said, as if he was trying it out. Her name came off his tongue like honey. She wished she had not invited him to call her by it.

"It smells good in here," he said conversationally and then looked around with interest. "It's quaint, exactly what I would expect an Italian kitchen to look like. That stone wall must be original to the house."

She felt tongue-tied but managed to squeak, "Don't be fooled by its charm. This house is three hundred years old. And it can be quite cranky."

"I think I noticed the crankiness in the shower just now," he said.

"I warned you about that." She did not want to be thinking about him in the shower, *again*.

"No big deal. Woke me up, though. The water was pouring out and then stopped, and then poured out again. I'll have a look at it for you, if you want."

"No," she said, proudly and firmly. She did not need to give herself the idea there was a man she could rely on to help her. "You are a guest in this house. I have already called the plumber, but I'm afraid with the renovation at the villa, my house is not a priority for him."

"I don't mind having a look at it."

Some longing shivered along her spine, which she straightened, instantly. "Signor, this house is three hundred years old. If you start looking at all the things wrong with it, I'm afraid you will not have time to do the job you came here to do. So, please, no, I can manage."

He looked faintly skeptical about her ability—or maybe the ability of any woman who was alone—to manage a three-hundred-year-old house, but wisely, he said nothing.

She dished out soup from the stove, gestured to the bread, took a seat across from him. She felt as if she was sitting rigidly upright, like a recent graduate from charm school.

"Relax," he said softly, "I won't bite you."

She was appalled that her discomfort was so transparent.

"Bite me?" she squeaked. She was also appalled at the picture that sprang to mind. And that it involved the cranky shower!

"It's American slang. It means I won't hurt you."

Wouldn't he? It seemed to her Connor Benson was the kind of man who hurt women without meaning to, and she didn't mean by attacking them outside the bedroom door in the morning, either. He was the kind of man who could make a woman think heated thoughts or dream naive and romantic dreams that he would not stick around to fulfill.

"This morning excepted," he growled.

"You didn't hurt me!"

"Not physically. I can tell you're nervous around me now."

She could feel the color climbing up her face. She wanted to deny that, and couldn't. Instead, she changed the subject. "How was your day?"

"Uneventful," he said. "I met with Nico and had an initial look around. It's a very beautiful village."

"Thank you. I like it very much." Her voice sounded stilted. What was wrong with her? Well, she'd married young. Giorgio had been her only boyfriend. She was not accustomed to this kind of encounter. "Would you like wine?"

"I'm not much of a drinker."

"You might like to try this one. It's one of Nico's best, from his Calanetti vineyard."

"All right," he said. She suspected he had said yes to help her relax, not because he really wanted the wine.

The wine was on the counter. Isabella was glad her back was to him, because she struggled with getting it open. But finally, she was able to turn back and pour him a glass. She could feel a dewy bead of sweat on her forehead. She blew on her bangs in case they were sticking.

He sipped it carefully as she sat back down. "It's really good. What would you say? *Buono?*"

"Yes, *buono.* Nico's vineyard is one of the pride and joys of our region." She took a sip of wine. And then another. It occurred to her neither of them were eating the soup.

Suddenly, it all felt just a little too cozy. Perhaps she should not have insisted on the wine. She took rather too large a gulp and set down her glass.

It was time to get down to business. "I will provide a simple supper like this, Mondays to Saturdays, the same days that I work. On Sunday, I do not. I provide breakfast every day, but I don't usually leave a tray by the bedroom door."

"I wouldn't risk that again, either," he said drily. She had the uncomfortable feeling he was amused by her.

"It's not a hotel," she said sternly, "so I don't make beds."

"Understood." Did he intentionally say that with a military inflection, as if he was a lower rank being addressed by a superior? Was he perceiving her as bossy?

Given how she wanted to keep everything formal between them, wouldn't that be a good thing?

"I also do not provide laundry service." Thank goodness. She could not even imagine touching his intimate things. "I have a washing machine through that door that you are welcome to use. There is a laundry service in the village if you prefer. Except for sheets, which I do once a week. I provide fresh towels every day."

"I can do my own sheets, thanks."

"All right. Yes. That's fine. The common areas of the house are yours to use if you want to watch television or cook your own meals, or put things in the refrigerator."

The thought of him in her space made her

take another rather large and fortifying sip of the wine.

"I don't watch television," he told her, "and I'm accustomed to preparing my own meals. I don't want you to feel put out by me. I can tell it is a bit of an imposition for you having a man in your house."

He was toying with the stem of his wineglass. He put it to his lips and took a long sip, watching her.

She tilted her chin at him, took a sip of her own wine. "What would make you say that? It's no imposition at all, Signor Benson."

Her heart was beating hard in her throat. He shrugged and lifted his wineglass to his lips again, watched her over the rim.

She might as well not have bothered denying it was any kind of imposition for her. She could feel her discomfort snaking along her spine, and he was not the kind of man you could hide things from.

"Connor, please," he said. "We're not very formal where I come from."

"Connor," she agreed. He had caught on that she was being too formal. Didn't he know it would protect them both? But she said his name anyway, even though it felt as if she was losing ground fast. She was using his first name. It felt as though she was agreeing, somehow, to dance with the devil.

But the question was, was the devil in him, or was it in her?

"And where are you from?" she asked. This was to prove to him she was not at all formal and stuffy and could hold a polite conversation with the best of them. She hoped it would not appear as if she was desperately eager for details about him, which she was not! She still had not touched her soup. Neither had he.

"I'm from Texas," he said.

"I thought the accent was like that of a cowboy."

He laughed at that. His laughter was deep and engaging, relaxing some of the constant hardness from his face, and she found herself staring at him.

"Ma'am—"

"Isabella," she reminded him.

"Isabella—"

Him saying her name, in that drawl, made her feel the same as if she had drunk a whole bottle of wine from the Calanetti vineyard instead of taken a few sips out of her glass.

Well, actually, her glass was empty, and so was his. He noticed, and tipped the wine out over both their glasses.

"Most people hear that drawl and automatically lower my intelligence by twenty points or so."

"I can tell you are a very intelligent man," she said seriously.

"I was just trying to make the point that regional accents can lead to judgments in the United States. Like you thinking I'm a cowboy. I'm about the farthest thing from a cowboy that you'll ever see."

"Oh! I thought everybody from Texas was a cowboy."

He laughed again. "You and the rest of the world. I grew up in a very poor neighborhood in Corpus Christi, which is a coastal city. I started picking up a bit of work at the shipyards when I was about eleven, and occasionally cattle would come through, but that's the closest I came to any real cowboys."

"Eleven?" she said, horrified. "That is very young to be working."

Something in his expression became guarded. He lifted a shoulder. "I was big for my age. No one asked how old I was."

"But why were you working at eleven?" she pressed.

For a moment, he looked as though he might not answer. Then he said quietly, "My mom was a single parent. It was pretty hand-to-mouth at times. I did what I could to help."

"Was your mom a widow?" she asked. She and Giorgio had not had children, though she had wanted to, even with Giorgio's prognosis. Now she wondered, from the quickly veiled pain in Connor's face, if that wouldn't have been a selfish thing, indeed, to try and raise a child or children without the benefit of a father.

"No," he said gruffly. "She wasn't a widow. She found herself pregnant at sixteen and abandoned by my father, whom she would never name. Her own family turned their backs on her. They said she brought shame on them by being pregnant."

"Your poor mother. Her own family turned away from her?" She thought of her family's reaction to the news she was going to marry Giorgio.

Life has enough heartbreak, her mother had said. *You have to invite one by marrying a dying man?*

Isabella could have pointed out to her mother that she should be an expert on heartbreak, since Isabella's father, with his constant infidelities, had broken her heart again and again and again. One thing about Giorgio? He was sweetly and strongly loyal. He would *never* be like that.

But it had seemed unnecessarily cruel to point that out to her mother, and so she had said nothing. And even though they were not happy with her choice, Isabella's family had not abandoned her. At least not physically.

Connor lifted a shoulder. "My mother is an amazing woman. She managed to keep me in line and out of jail through my wild youth. That couldn't have been easy."

"I'm sure it was not," Isabella said primly.

He grinned as if he had enjoyed every second of his wild youth. "Then I joined up."

"Joined up?"

"I joined the navy as soon as I was old enough."

"How old is that?"

"Seventeen."

She drew in her breath sharply.

"I served in the regular navy for two years, and then I was drawn to the SEALs."

"SEALs? What is this?"

"It stands for sea, air, land. It's an arm of the navy. Combat divers."

She could tell there was a bit more to it than what he was saying.

"And your mother? Was she heartbroken when you left her to join the military?"

He smiled wryly. "Not at all. Once she didn't have to expend all of her energy keeping me fed and in line, she married a rich guy she cleaned for. She seems deliriously happy and has produced a number of little half siblings for me."

"You adore them," Isabella guessed.

"Guilty."

"I'm glad your mother found happiness."

"Me, too, though her luck at love has made her think everyone should try it."

"And shouldn't they?" Isabella found herself asking softly.

He rolled his shoulders, and something shut down in his face. "A man who seeks danger with the intensity and trajectory of a heat-seeking missile is not exactly a good bet in the love department. I've seen lots of my buddies go down that road. They come home cold and hard and damaged. Normal life and domestic duties seem unbearably dull after the adrenaline rush of action."

"That sounds very lonely," Isabella offered. *And like a warning.* Which she dutifully noted.

Connor studied her for a moment. Whatever had opened between them closed like a door slamming shut. He pushed back from the table abruptly. "Lonely? Not at all," he insisted coolly. "Thank you for dinner."

But he hadn't eaten dinner. After a moment, she cleared his uneaten soup off the table and cleaned up the kitchen.

Really, he had let her know in every way possible that any interest in him would not be appreciated.

After putting her small kitchen in order, she retreated to her office. She hesitated only a moment before she looked up navy seals on the internet. She felt guilty as sin doing it, but it did not stop her.

It was actually SEALs, she discovered, and they were not just combat divers. Sometimes called Frogmen because they were equally adept in the water or on land, they were one of the most elite, and secretive, commando forces in the world.

Only a very few men, of the hundreds who tried, could make it through their rigorous training program.

Isabella could tell from what she read that Connor had led a life of extreme adventure and excitement. He was, unfortunately, the larger-than-life kind of man who intrigued.

But he had told her with his own words

what he was. Cold and hard and damaged. She was all done rescuing men.

Rescuing men? something whispered within her. *But you never felt you were rescuing Giorgio. Never. You did it all for love.*

But suddenly, sickeningly, she just wasn't that sure what her motives had been in marrying a man with such a terrible prognosis.

And fairly or not, looking at her husband and her marriage through a different lens felt as if it was entirely the fault of Connor Benson.

Even knowing she had been quite curious enough for one night, she decided to look up one more thing. She put in the name Itus Security. There was a picture of a very good-looking man named Justin Arnold. He was the CEO of the company. Beside his picture was one of Connor, who was the chief of operations. There was a list of services they offered, and a number of testimonials from very high-profile clients.

Their company was named after the Greek god of protection, Itus, and their mission statement was, "As in legend, Itus is sworn to protect the innocent from those who would do them harm."

Intrigued, she went and read the mythol-

ogy around Itus. A while later, Isabella shut
off the computer and squared her shoulders.

A month. Connor Benson was going to be
under her roof for a month. After one day,
she was feeling a terrible uneasiness, as if he
could, with just his close proximity, change
everything about her, even the way she looked
at her past.

"I have to avoid him," she whispered to
herself. And it felt as if her very survival depended on that. She went to bed and set her
alarm for very early. She could put out his
breakfast things and leave the house without
even seeing him tomorrow. There were always things to do at school. Right now, she
was preparing her class to perform a song
and skit at the annual spring fete, and she had
props to make, simple costumes to prepare.

She had a feeling with Connor under her
roof and her badly needing her schoolroom to
hide out in and something to distract from the
uncomfortable feelings she was experiencing, she was about to produce the best song
and skit the good citizens of Monte Calanetti
had ever seen!

CHAPTER THREE

Connor retreated to his room, annoyed with himself. He was not generally so chatty. What moment of madness had made him say yes to that wine? And why had so very little of it made him feel so off balance?

Intoxicated.

Maybe it hadn't been the wine, but just sharing a simple meal with a beautiful woman in the quintessential Italian kitchen, with its old stone walls and its deep windows open to the breeze, that had brought his guard down.

He had told Isabella things he had not told people he'd worked with for twenty years. Justin knew about his hardscrabble upbringing on the wrong side of Corpus Christi, but no one else did.

The soft look in Isabella's eyes as he had told her had actually made him feel not that he wanted to tell her less, but as though he

wanted to tell her more, as if his every secret
would be safe with her.

As if he had carried a burden alone for
way too long.

"Stop it," Connor snapped grimly at himself. He acknowledged he was tired beyond
reason. You didn't unload on a woman like
her. She, cute little schoolteacher that she was,
wouldn't be able to handle it, to hold up to it.
She'd buried her husband and that had sent
her into full retreat. That's why someone so
gorgeous was still unmarried six years later.

So there would be no more wine tastings
over supper that loosened his tongue. No
more suppers, in fact. Tomorrow, rested, his
first duty would be to find a nice little place
to eat supper every night.

With none of the local wines. That one tonight had seemed to have some beautiful Tuscan enchantment built right into it.

And if avoiding her at dinner proved to be
not enough defense, he would go in search of
another place to stay.

Not that he wanted to hurt her feelings.

"The Cat does not worry about people's
feelings," he said, annoyed with himself.
What he needed to do was deal with the
exhaustion first. He peeled off his clothes

and rolled into bed and slept, but not before grumpily acknowledging how hungry he was.

Connor awoke very early. He knew where he was this time. Again, he could hear the sounds of someone trying to be very quiet. He rolled over and looked at his bedside clock.

Five a.m. What the heck? He had the awful thought Isabella might have gotten up so early to make him breakfast. That made him feel guilty since he knew she had a full day of work to put in. Guilt was as unusual for him as worrying about feelings. Still, he needed to tell her not to bother.

He slipped on a pair of lightweight khakis and pulled a shirt over his head, and went downstairs to the kitchen.

She had her back to him.

"Isabella?"

She shrieked and turned, hand to her throat.

"Sorry," he said, "I've startled you again."

She dropped her hand from her throat. "No, you didn't," she said, even though it was more than obvious she had been very startled.

"Whatever. I think we've got to quit meeting like this."

The expression must have lost something in the translation, because she only looked annoyed as she turned back to the counter. "I just wasn't expecting you to be up so early."

"I wasn't expecting you up this early."

"I'm preparing for the spring festival," she said. "I have extra work to do at school."

"And extra work to do here, because of me?"

She glanced over her shoulder at him, and then looked quickly back at what she was doing, silent.

"I wanted to let you know not to fuss over me. A box of cereal on the table and some milk in the fridge is all I need in the morning. And coffee."

"I'll just show you how to use the coffeemaker then—"

He smiled. "I've made coffee on every continent and in two dozen different countries. I can probably figure it out."

She looked very pretty this morning. Her hair was scraped back in a ponytail. It made her look, again, younger than he knew her to be. The rather severe hairstyle also showed off the flawless lines of her face. She had on a different sleeveless dress, and her lips had a hint of gloss on them that made them look full and faintly pouty.

"All right then," she said, moving away from the coffeemaker. "So, no breakfast?"

"I don't need supper tonight, either. I'm kind of used to fending for myself."

And he did not miss the look of relief on her face.

So he added, "Actually, I probably won't need dinner any night. Instead of letting you know if I won't be here, how about if I let you know if I will?"

The look on her face changed to something else, quickly masked. It only showed him the wisdom of his decision. The little schoolteacher *wanted* someone to look after, and it would be better if she did not get any ideas that it was going to be him!

"I actually like to swim before I eat anything in the morning. This is the perfect time of day for swimming."

"It's not even light out."

"I know. That's what makes it perfect."

Whenever he could, Connor had begun every morning of his life for as long as he could remember with a swim. That affinity for the water had, in part, been what made him such a good fit for the SEALs. But when he left the SEALs, it was the only place he had found where he could outrun—or outswim, as it were—his many demons. Despite Justin's well-meaning advice to take a rest from it, Connor simply could not imagine life without the great stress relief and fitness provided by the water.

"You'll wake people up."

"Actually, Nico invited me to use the pool at his private garden in the villa, but I'd prefer to swim in the river."

"The river? It's very cold at this time of year."

"Perfect."

"And probably dangerous."

"I doubt it, but I already warned you about men like me and danger."

"Yes, you did," she whispered. "There's a place on the river where the boys swim in the summer. Would you like me to show it to you?"

"You aren't trying to protect me from danger, are you, Isabella?" he asked quietly.

"That would be a very foolish undertaking, I'm sure," she said, a little stain that confirmed his suspicions moving up her cheeks. "It's hard to find, the place where the boys swim. That's all."

"Yes, please, then, show it to me," he heard himself saying, though he had no doubt he could find good places to swim all by himself. He didn't want to hurt her pride. "Yes, I'd like that very much."

And so he found himself, with dawn smudging the air, painting the medieval skyline of Monte Calanetti in magnificence, walking down twisting streets not yet touched by the light beside Isabella to the river.

And enjoying the pink-painted splendor of the moment way more than he had a right to.

Isabella contemplated what moment of madness had made the words slip from her mouth that she would show Connor the way to the river. By getting up so early, she'd been trying to avoid him this morning.

Instead, she was walking through the still darkened streets of Monte Calanetti with him by her side.

And despite the pure madness that must have motivated her invitation, she would not have withdrawn it had she been given a chance. Because that moment, of unguarded impulse, had led to this one.

It was unexpectedly magical, the streets still dim, the brilliance of the dawn that was staining the sky above them not yet reaching into the cracks and crevices of the town.

The occasional light was blinking on in the houses and businesses they passed.

Isabella was intensely aware of how it felt to have this man walk beside her. He was so big, his presence commanding. He had gone back up to his room for a moment, and when he came down he carried a small black bag and had a white towel strung around his neck.

He had a way of walking—shoulders back, stride long and confident and calm—that gave a sense that he owned the earth and he knew it. Isabella had never felt unsafe in Monte Calanetti, but she was aware, walking beside him, of feeling immensely protected.

"I can't believe the light," he said. "I've never seen anything like it."

"It's part of what makes Tuscany famous, that quality of light. Artists throng here for that."

"How would you say this in Italian?" he said, making a sweeping gesture that took in everything—the amazing light and the twisting streets, still in shadows, dawn beginning to paint the rooflines in gold.

She thought a moment. Wasn't this exactly what she had longed to do and had decided was dangerous? The morning was too beautiful to fight with herself, to be petty about what she would and wouldn't give. She would give him a few words, nothing more.

"In tutto il suo splendore," Isabella said.

He repeated it, rolling the words off his tongue. Mixed with his drawl and the deepness of his voice, it was very charming.

"And the translation?" he asked her.

"In glory."

"Ah," he said. "Perfect."

After that neither of them attempted conversation, but the quiet was comfortable between them as they moved down the narrow streets. It gave a sense of walking toward the light as they left the last of the buildings behind and followed the road past the neat row of vineyards that followed the undulating green of the hills.

"There it is," she said, finally, pointing at the ribbon of river that had become visible up ahead of them. "When you come to the bridge, turn right and follow the river. You'll see a tire suspended on a rope where the boys swim."

"Thank you. *Grazie.*"

"You're welcome." She should have turned back toward the town, but she did not. She recognized a reluctance to leave the simple glory of this moment behind. He must have felt that, too.

"Come with me." His voice was husky.

Come with him? Where?

"Swimming?" she asked. Her voice felt very squeaky. It felt as if he had asked something far graver. To tangle their lives together, to follow the thread of magic that had led them through the town in the enchanted light of early morning.

When he said nothing, she rushed to fill the silence. "I couldn't possibly. I don't know how to swim. The water will be cold. I—I—I don't have proper bathing wear."

"Don't come this far and not at least put your feet in the water."

It felt as if he was saying something else altogether. He was inviting her to wake up instead of sleeping. He was inviting her to really live instead of going through the motions of living.

"I have to tell you a little secret," she confessed. "I've never learned to swim because I am a little bit afraid of the water."

"All the more reason to say yes instead of no," he said.

It occurred to her Connor Benson was that kind of man. Being with him would challenge you to be more than you had been before. She had always been perfectly content with who she was before!

"Maybe another time," she said uneasily.

"Putting your feet in the water is the first step to swimming, to overcoming that fear."

"It's not as if it's a crippling fear—it's not as if it changes my life," she said defensively, already sorry she'd confided in him that she was afraid.

"Fear can be a gift," he said, his voice calm and low. "It can show you that you are in very real danger. But an irrational fear can change your life in ways you don't even understand. If you give in to it, it can expand. So, one day you're afraid of swimming, the next you're afraid of everything."

Did he see her as afraid of everything? And how much truth was there in that? She looked at the safe little world she had created for herself. Maybe, even if it was annoying, maybe he was right. She needed to stretch just a tiny bit out of her comfort zone.

What would it hurt to get her feet wet?

"All right," she whispered, and was rewarded with a tentative smile. The smile put the dawn to shame and warned her exploring new territories and experiences was always going to be fraught with hidden dangers.

That's why she had chosen life as a schoolteacher in a small town. Her choices had given her a life with a reassuring sameness to everything that made her feel safe and secure.

Though in this amazing dawn, she saw things in a new and less flattering light. Had she allowed herself to become utterly boring? Apparently. Apparently she had become the kind of woman who you could tell in a single glance was a schoolteacher.

They came to the bridge and stood on it for a moment. The water was flowing underneath it like liquid gold, stained by the rising sun. They stood there in silence, watching morning mist rise off the vineyards all around them.

"Everyone should know how to swim," he said sternly, as if he was deliberately moving away from the magic of the shared moment, as if he was making sure she was not mistaken about his motivations in asking her to join him.

"Really? Why?"

He frowned at her, as if the question was too silly to deserve an answer.

"Most of the world's population, including

you, lives near some sort of body of water. You could be in a boat that capsizes. You could fall in."

"I suppose," she agreed, but looking at him, she recognized what was at his very core. He protected people. It was more than evident that was his vocation and his calling. His shoulders were huge and broad, but broad enough to carry the weight of the whole world?

He broke her gaze, as if he knew she had seen something of him that he did not want her to see. Connor moved off the bridge and found a path worn deep by the feet of hundreds of hot little boys over many, many years.

The path was steep in places, and her footwear—a pair of flimsy sandals, fine for town—was not very good for scrambling over rocks.

"Oh," she gasped at one point, when she nearly fell.

He turned, took it all in in a breath, and his hands found her waist and encircled it. He lifted her easily over the rough spot and set her down. But his hands remained around her waist for just a hair too long, and then he turned away just a hair too quickly.

Her sensation of being with a man who

would protect her with his life, if need be, strengthened.

It made her feel exquisitely feminine to be the one being looked after, for a change. Giorgio had never looked after her. It had always been the other way around.

A touch of guilt rippled along the perfect mirrored surface of the morning. But it evaporated like the mist rising all around them as they arrived at the swimming hole. Her awareness of Connor seemed to fill up every crack and crevice in her, just as sunlight would be filling every crack and crevice as it poured into the town.

The river widened here, gurgling on both sides of a pool that was large and placid. A tree leaned over it, and from a sturdy branch, a tire swung on a frayed rope.

Connor kicked off his shoes and shucked his trousers and his shirt and stood before her much as he had yesterday, totally unselfconscious in bathing trunks that were the same cut and style as his underwear had been, and every bit as sexy. He bent over his bag for a moment and fished out something that he held loosely in his left hand.

He stepped to the water's edge.

"Is it cold?" she asked.

"Oh, yeah," he said with deep pleasure. He reached back his right hand for her. "It's a bit slippery."

Crazy to accept that invitation, but really, it was much too late to stop accepting the crazy invitations now. She kicked out of her sandals and reached out. His hand closed around hers, and he tugged her gently to the water's edge. She was not sure anything in her entire life had felt as right as accepting the strength of that hand, feeling it close around her own, with a promise of strength and protection.

"The first step to swimming," he encouraged her.

She stuck a toe in, shrieked and pulled it back out swiftly. She tried to loosen her hand from his, but he just laughed and held tight until she put her toe back in the water.

"Come on," he said, patiently. "Just try it."

And so, her hand held firmly in his, she stepped into the icy cold water and felt her eyes go round. The mud on the bottom oozed up between her toes.

It felt wondrous. She didn't feel the least bit afraid. He tugged her hand and smiled. What could she do? She could say yes to life. Isabella bunched up her skirt in her other hand and lifted it. The morning air on her naked thighs felt exquisite. She saw his eyes move there, to where she had lifted her skirt out of the water, and felt slightly vindicated by the flash of deep masculine heat she saw in them. That was not the look one gave a boring schoolteacher.

He led her deeper into the water—it crept up to her calves and to her knees—and he smiled at her squeal that was part protest and mostly delight. And then she was laughing.

The laughter felt as if it was bubbling up from a hidden stream deep within her; it had been trapped and now it was set free.

Connor was staring at her, and his gaze added to the sense of heightened awareness. She was entering another world, a foreign land of sensation, his hand so warm and strong guiding her, the cold water tugging on her feet and her bare calves, licking at her knees, storming her senses. She was not sure she had ever felt so exquisitely and fully alive.

Something sizzled in the air between them, as real as getting a jolt from a loose wire. Connor Benson was looking at her lips. She allowed herself to look at his.

A knife-edged awareness surged through her. If she took one tiny step toward him, she knew he would kiss her.

Was this what she had given up when she had chosen Giorgio? Was this what her mother had tried to tell her she would miss? The thought was an unexpected dark spot in the brightness of her unleashed spirit.

She felt the laughter dry up within her, and Isabella let go of Connor's hand and took a step back instead of toward him.

"What?" he asked.

She backed away from his touch, from the exquisite intoxication of his closeness. It was clouding her judgment. It was making her crazy.

Ma sei pazzo, she chided herself inside her own head, backing away from the delicious craziness that beckoned to her.

But he did not allow her to escape. For every step back she took, he took one forward, until she was up against the slippery bank and could not move for fear of falling in the water. He came to her and lifted her chin, looked deeply into her eyes. "What?" he asked again, softly.

She could feel the strength in his hands, the calm in his eyes. She could smell the scents of him and of the morning mingling. She could lean toward all of this...

But she didn't.

"Nothing," she said. "I have to go. I can't—"

Can't what? she asked herself. Enjoy life? Be open to new experiences? She broke away from his gaze—a gaze that seemed to know all her secrets, to strip her of everything she had regarded as truth before. She gathered her skirt, shoved by him, waded up the river to where it was easy to find the bank and left the water.

"You can use my towel to dry off your feet," he called.

She did that. She grabbed his towel and her shoes and found a dry place on the bank to sit and towel off her feet.

She dared to glance at him. He stood, watching her. He was so extraordinarily attractive, those strong legs set in the water, the morning light playing with the features of his face, so comfortable in his own skin. Italians had an expression about men like this.

Sa il fatto suo.

He knows what he is about. He knows himself.

And then this man who knew himself so well, who knew his every strength and his every weakness, lifted a shoulder, dismissing her. He dipped the mask and snorkel he held in his left hand into the water. He slipped them on, resting them on his forehead. Then he casually saluted her, adjusted the mask and snorkel, and dived neatly into the water and disappeared.

She held her breath. Where on earth had he gone? It seemed as if he could not possibly be down there for that long without something having happened. Was he tangled in a branch under the water? Had he hit his head on a rock?

But then the water broke, at the far edge of the pool, where faster water fed it. He broke the surface, and without looking back began to swim against the current.

It would always be like this if you were with a man like him, Isabella told herself sternly. *You would always wonder what danger he had managed to find.*

And still, she could not tear her eyes away from him. She watched in utter amazement as Connor propelled himself through the water. His strength and his grace were utterly awe-inspiring. It was as if there was no current at all, his body cutting through the water at high speed. If she didn't know better, she would think he had flippers on, but no flippers had come out of that bag. She watched him swim until he reached a bend in the river, swam around it and disappeared.

She finished drying her feet and put her shoes on. It was harder navigating the tricky path back to the bridge without him.

But it was what she had to do. She had to navigate without him—she had to go back to the way her life had been before they took that walk into a world of enchantment, this world where fears evaporated like the morning mist was evaporating under the Tuscan sun.

Isabella had to be who she was before.

A few minutes did not alter the course of an entire life.

But she of all people should know that was not true, because the entire course of her life had been altered the second she had said *I do* to Giorgio.

And it felt like the worst kind of sin that these few minutes this morning had filled her with regret, for the first time, at what the choice to say those words had made her miss in life.

But one thing about saying that to Giorgio? If she ever did say those words to a man again—and that was a big, big *if*—it would be to one who would grow old with her.

And there would never, ever be a guarantee of that with a man like Connor Benson.

The river was amazing to swim in, and Connor quickly made morning swims a part of his Monte Calanetti routine. His time in the military had made him move toward a structured approach to life. He loved routine and order. From firsthand experience, Connor knew when the world turned to chaos—which it could do in the blink of an eye—that was when an investment in discipline paid dividends.

And so now he developed a schedule for his days. He rose early, before Isabella was up, walked to the river and swam against the current in the cold water until his muscles ached but his mind was sharply clear and focused.

It was all working out quite nicely. By the time he returned, Isabella had left for work.

Isabella. The clear mind made Connor uncomfortably aware, especially after that magical morning together, that this time Isabella could well be the chaos waiting to unfold in his life.

And that kind of chaos was way more dangerous than the sudden crack of a sniper's rifle, or a bomb going off on the side of the road.

Oh, she seemed innocent enough, the last place a man would expect chaos to come from, but that would be a man who had not felt her hand close around his, who had not heard her unexpected shriek of delighted laughter split the silence of the morning as her toes touched ice-cold water. That would be a man who had not, for one crazy, glorious moment, looked at her lips and wanted to taste the promise of them, wanted to see if they tasted like the nectar of life itself.

The answer was simple. No more dawn encounters. No more walking through streets so quiet he could hear her dress swishing against her bare legs, no more putting his hands around her narrow waist to lift her over the rocky parts of the trail. No more wading in icy cold water with her. No more encouraging her to explore the world of sensation.

And especially no more looking at the sweet plumpness of her lips!

A man—one not as disciplined as Connor knew himself to be—could live to see the light that had come on in Isabella's face that morning by the river.

And so, he was avoiding her. And his avoidance had helped him develop a routine that he was comfortable with. There were no more tongue-loosening little chats over wine, and no more shocking morning encounters in the hallway or kitchen, and most of all, no more morning strolls through a predawn town.

Isabella seemed to enjoy routine as much as he himself did, and so it was proving easy to avoid her. He, an expert on figuring out people's habits, had her routine down pat in no time. It fit perfectly with his lifestyle.

By the time he returned from his early morning swims, Isabella was gone. He used the kitchen and did his laundry when she was at school. A lot of his work could be done on his computer, and he took advantage of her absence and the coolness on the lower floors of her house to do that when she was not there.

When she was at home in the evenings, he went out to eat and did reconnaissance. It was cooler then, anyway, and he made sure never to be back until her house lights—and her bedroom light, which he could see from the street—were out.

Even with all that effort, it was hard to ignore the fact he was sharing a house with a woman. No, it seemed his avoidance strategy had made *more* awareness, not less, tingle along his spine. Her little touches were ev-

erywhere in that house: an exquisite painting, a fresh vase of flowers, the smell of toast
and coffee in the morning. Her scent was in
the air.

And by now it had become apparent to him
that all the while he was congratulating himself on his avoidance strategy, the truth was
it was so successful because she was avoiding him!

By the fifth day of living under her roof,
after succeeding with zero encounters of the
Isabella-in-person kind, Connor was not at all
sure what his success meant, because he was
fairly certain he had never been more aware
of another person.

Connor came into the house. It was much
earlier than he usually arrived in the afternoon, but he felt a need to change clothes before he went and found a place to eat tonight.
It had been another scorching day in Monte
Calanetti and he thought he might head to the
river for the second time that day.

He paused and listened. Had he managed
to get in before she got home from school?

Today, for the first time, he realized he
had not been successful in avoiding sharing
the house with his appealing roommate. He

could hear the one and only shower running upstairs.

Well, that was okay. He would nip into his room and get his swim things and a change of clothes. Isabella wouldn't even know he'd been in the space. The thought of bumping into her in the hallway, fresh out of the shower, made him hurriedly gather his swim things from his room.

His escape was nearly complete when the sound of an explosion, followed by a woman's shriek of terror, came from the bathroom. There was a loud *thunk*.

And then there was the worst thing of all.

Complete and utter silence.

CHAPTER FOUR

WITHOUT EVEN THINKING, doing what came as naturally to him as breathing, Connor threw down his things and ran into the hallway, straight toward the now silent bathroom.

"Isabella? Are you okay?"

There was no answer. He pounded on the door. There was still no answer. He tried the door. It was locked.

"Isabella?"

When there was still no answer, he put his shoulder to the door. The old wood cracked with ease and the door fell open.

He was hit in the face by water. He threw his hands up over his face and peered out between two fingers. Water was spewing out of the pipe where the showerhead had been, going in every direction, drenching the walls in water. The showerhead was on the floor under the sink.

Isabella was on the floor, soaked. The shower curtain had been ripped from its rod, and it was draped across her naked body. Turning his back to the spraying water to protect her from the worst of it, he crouched down beside her. Her head was bleeding and a lump was already rising.

"Isabella," he said, touching her wet arm.

She opened her eyes, dazed. Her brows knit as she looked at him in confusion.

"I—I—I don't know what happened."

"I think the showerhead blew off and hit you." He rose quickly, turned off the water at the handle, and then crouched back beside her.

"Please don't tell me, 'I told you so.'" Her eyes were wide on his face, all those greens and golds mixed together like the shades of an exotic flower.

"I won't."

"I should have let you fix it when the plumber wouldn't come. Didn't want to be dependent." Her voice was slightly slurred. It sounded like a bit of a confession. Her eyes suddenly widened even more. "Are you in my bathroom?"

"Yes, I'm afraid so."

She went very still. If it was possible, she grew whiter. "Am I naked?" she whispered.

"Ah, I'm afraid so."

"I have never been so mortified." She clenched her eyes shut as if she was hoping when she opened them this would all go away.

"Now we're even," he said, trying valiantly to put her at ease. "Though I think I've mentioned before that we should stop meeting like this."

She groaned weakly—at his attempt at humor or because of pain and humiliation, he wasn't so certain.

"We're not even," she decided. "We'd be even if you had ever been embarrassed about being unclothed, which I suspect you never have been."

He didn't say anything.

"In your whole life."

He still didn't say anything.

"Have you?" she demanded.

"Uh, well, you're not exactly unclothed. You must have pulled down the shower curtain when you came out of the shower enclosure. You're decent."

"My shower curtain is transparent," she said through clenched teeth.

"I'm not looking."

Of course her eyes flew open just as he looked. "Just for injuries!"

She clenched her eyes tightly shut again.

"I'm going to help you get up."

"No, you aren't!" She tried to tuck the transparent shower curtain tighter around her. It had the unfortunate result of becoming even more transparent.

"Ah, yes, I am," he said, keeping his eyes on her face. Chaos had struck. And all that discipline was paying off, after all. He could look just at her face. Couldn't he?

"I can get up myself." She wiggled ineffectually this way and that, trying to figure out how to get up on the slippery floor and keep the small protection of the shower curtain around her at the same time. She gave up with a sigh.

He reached out to help her.

"Don't touch me." She slapped at his hand, but it was halfhearted.

"You can trust me." His hand closed around hers, and this time she surrendered. "I have pretty extensive first-aid training."

"Yes, I know."

He lifted an eyebrow at her.

"I read about it. On the internet. The SEALs."

"Oh." She had read about what he'd done for a living. He contemplated that.

"Not that I was spying."

"No, of course not."

"Just intrigued."

"Ah."

"It seems like you have done very dangerous things."

"Yes."

Her voice suddenly went very soft. "Things that make a man very lonely."

Her eyes felt as if they were looking deep within him, as if she could see his soul, as if she could see the vast emptiness that was there. Her hand tightened marginally on his.

"Maybe," he said, telling himself he was only agreeing because he didn't want her to get riled up.

"I feel lonely, too, sometimes." And then, just like that, she was crying.

"Hey." He patted her shoulder clumsily, realized how very naked she was and pulled his hand away. He stared at it as if it was burning.

She seemed to realize how awkward this situation really was. "You need to leave me alone," she sobbed. "I'm not even dressed."

What *wasn't* happening? He wasn't leaving her alone. What *was* happening? He was going to try and make her okay with this.

"Don't worry about it," he said, pulling his attention away from his hand and ordering himself to buck up. "You've had a bit of a shock. People say and do things they wouldn't normally say or do. I'm a trained professional. I deal with stuff like this all the time."

Even as she scrubbed furiously at her tearstained face, she looked dubious. She slid a look down at her thin covering of a shower curtain. "Like a doctor?"

"Sort of," he agreed.

"And you deal with unclothed, crying, lonely women who have been assaulted by exploding showers? All the time?"

"I just meant I deal with the unexpected." He tried for a soothing note in the face of her voice rising a bit shrilly. "It's what I'm trained to do. Let's get you up off the floor."

He reached for the nearest towel rack and tugged a towel off it, and then, as an afterthought, another one. He put both of them on top of her, trying to fasten them, without much success, around the sopping, slippery, transparent shower curtain.

Tucking the thick white terry towels around her as best he could, he slipped his arm under her shoulder and lifted her to a little dressing table bench. It was the first time he had touched her since he had held her hand at the pool in the river. Awareness quivered along his spine, but he could not give in to that. He needed to be professional right now, as he never had been before.

Connor guided Isabella to sitting and tucked the towels a little tighter around her.

Professional, he told himself grimly.

"Let's just have a look at that bump on your head." *That was good*, he told himself of his neutral tone.

"Why are you lonely?" he heard himself growl as he parted her hair and dabbed at the bump with a wet cloth.

What was professional about that? *Distracting her*, Connor told himself. He turned from her for a moment and opened the medicine chest over her sink. He found iodine and cotton balls.

"I suppose you find me pathetic," she said.

Distracting her would have been talking about anything—the upcoming royal wedding, the grape crops—not probing her personal tragedies.

She grimaced as he found the cut on her head and dabbed it.

"I don't find you pathetic," he told her. "You were married. Your husband died. It seems to me you would be lonely."

"Thank you," she said softly.

Leave it, he ordered himself. "I mean, of course I've wondered why such a beautiful woman would stay alone."

"You wondered about me?"

Just as she had wondered about him, going online to find out about the SEALs. All this curiosity between them was just normal, wasn't it? They were two strangers sharing a house. Naturally they would have questions.

"Did you love your husband that much?" Connor asked. "That you are prepared to stay lonely forever? To grieve him forever?"

"Yes," she said. It came out sounding like a hiccup. "Where there is deep grief, there was deep love."

And something about the way she said that made his radar go up. He realized he didn't believe her. It was none of his business. He ordered himself not to probe. He was, at heart, a soldier. He would always be a soldier. That's what he did. He obeyed orders.

So, why did he hear his own voice saying, in direct defiance of the command he had just given it, "Tell me about your husband."

It was not, as he would have liked himself to believe, to provide a distraction for her while he doctored her head.

"No one, least of all not my very traditional family, understood my decision to marry him," she said, sticking her chin up as if daring him to reach the same conclusion.

"Why's that?" he asked, keeping his voice carefully noncommittal.

"He was very ill when we married. We knew he was going to die."

He had to work to keep his face schooled.

"My mother was begging me, on the eve of my wedding, not to do it. She said, *Life has enough heartbreak—you have to invite one by marrying a dying man?*"

It seemed to Connor her mother had a point, but he didn't say anything. He pretended intense concentration on the small bump on her head.

"Giorgio was part of the fabric of my life from the first day I started school."

Connor could just picture her starting school: little dark pigtails, a pinafore dress, knee socks and a scraped knee.

Something that had never happened to him happened—he wondered what Isabella's daughter would look like, if she had one someday. He felt it was a tragedy that she had said no to her own little girl somewhere along the line.

"Giorgio was never good-looking." Isabella looked at Connor critically. He was pretty sure she found *him* good-looking, but not nearly as sure if she saw that as a good thing or a bad thing.

"He wasn't even good-looking as a child, though his eyes held such depths of beauty they took my breath away from the first moment I looked in their liquid dark depths."

He had to bite his tongue from saying cynically, *How very poetic*.

"He was always sickly—perhaps seeds of the illness that killed him had been growing since we were children."

Connor did not like the picture she was painting of the man she had married. Good grief. What had she been thinking?

She seemed to sense his judgment, because she tilted her chin at him. "He took the fact he was different from all the other boys and made that his greatest strength."

"Oh," he said flatly, not a question. But she took it as a question.

"Giorgio was able to use such a simple thing as a word to spin entire worlds, enchanted

kingdoms. He could see what others missed—
the pure magic in a ladybug's flight, the whole
universe residing in the center of an opening
flower. While other boys were crass and full
of frightening energy, Giorgio was sensitive
and sweetly contemplative."

Connor hoped he wasn't scowling. He himself had been one of those crass boys, full of
frightening energy.

"When he asked me to marry him, I didn't
even have to think about it, I just said yes."

What kind of man, knowing his prognosis
was fatal, would ask someone he supposedly
loved to share that with him?

"I've never even been on a real date. Giorgio was not well enough to go out for dinner,
or to the movies. Certainly not dancing."

She'd never been on a date? That last—
certainly not dancing — seemed to have been
offered with a bit of wistfulness.

"I still have the poems he wrote for me,
and the splendor of them is still wrenching
enough to make me weep."

Connor looked at her lips. If she hadn't
dated any other men, she probably hadn't
kissed any other men, either. He had the ir-
reverent feeling he could make her forget the
splendor of those poems in about twenty sec-

onds flat. He made himself focus on the small cut on her head.

"At sixteen I declared my love for him. At twenty I married him, over the protests of my entire family. He had already been diagnosed with his illness. At twenty-six I laid him to rest. In my heart is nothing but gratitude for the amazing time we had."

She seemed to be expecting him to say something, so he said, "Uh-huh," when what he really wanted to do was take her by those slender, very naked shoulders and shake some sense into her.

"Now in me is an empty place that nothing—and no one—can ever fill."

Her tale made Connor want to kiss the living daylights out of her, to wake her up from her trance, to show her maybe that empty place inside her could be filled. But he recognized he was treading on dangerous and unfamiliar ground if he thought he would be the one who was up to the challenge of filling her empty places. Isabella apparently liked the sensitive type. Which, if the way he felt about her husband was any indication, Connor most definitely was not. The man had been sick. That wasn't his fault. And yet Connor felt aggravated, as if Giorgio had taken advantage of Isabella's soft heart to give her a life of looking after him.

"You think I felt sorry for him," she gasped. "You think I didn't love him at all."

"Hey! I didn't say that."

"You didn't have to. I saw it in your face. You think I don't have a clue what love is."

He was the one who had told her to be observant, but he hadn't been expecting this. "I don't know what you think you saw in my face, but it wasn't that. You did not see that in *my* face, because you are looking at a person who truly does not have a clue what love is."

"Humph." She seemed unconvinced. She seemed unfairly angry at him.

"Maybe," he suggested carefully, "you said out loud the doubt you've been nursing inside since the day you married him."

With speed that took him by surprise, she smacked him hard, open-handed, across his face, hard enough to turn his head. He looked slowly back at her as she stood up. The towel fell to the ground, leaving only the shower curtain around her. Gathering her shower curtain, regal as Christina Rose could ever hope to be, as confident as the emperor with no clothes, Isabella got up and walked by him and out of the bathroom. He watched as she walked down the hallway to her bedroom, entered it, sent one damning look back at him and slammed the door.

Connor Benson stood frozen to the spot, absolutely stunned. He touched his face where her palm had met his cheek.

Jeez, for a little bit of a thing she packed a better wallop than a lot of men he'd known.

Isabella lay, wrapped in her shower curtain, on her bed in a pool of dampness and self-loathing. She could not believe she had struck Connor. She was going to have to apologize. It was so unlike her!

It was only because she had hit her head. He'd said it himself. She'd had a bit of a shock—people did and said things they wouldn't normally say under those circumstances.

Isabella would not normally confess all kinds of things to him. She had told him she was lonely in a moment of dazed weakness. It was also in a moment of dazed weakness that she had given in to his encouragement to talk about Giorgio.

What a mistake that had been. She had seen in Connor's face that he thought her marriage had been a sham.

Or was what he said more accurate? That

bump on the head had removed a filter she had been trying desperately to keep in place, and her own doubts, not Connor's, had spilled out of her.

She got up off the bed. Enough of the self-pity and introspection. Yes, she was lonely, but why had she confessed that to him instead of just looking after it herself?

People had to be responsible for themselves!

Tonight was a case in point. She had been invited to the sixteenth birthday party of one of her former students. As a teacher, she was often invited to her pupils' family events, but she rarely attended. So, who did she have to blame but herself if she was lonely?

It wasn't Connor's fault that he had made her aware of the loneliness as if it was a sharp shard of glass inside her.

She went to her closet and threw open the door. She wasn't going to the party as a demure little schoolteacher, either. She wasn't wearing a dress that would label her prim and tidy for all the world to see.

She was not dressing in a way that sent the message she was safe and boring, and not quite alive somehow.

Way at the back of the closet was a dress

she had bought a long time ago, on a holiday she had forced herself to take a year or two after Giorgio died. The purchase had really been the fault of one of those pushy sales-clerks who had brought her the dress, say-ing she had never seen a dress so perfect for someone.

It was the salesclerk's gushing that had made Isabella purchase the dress, which had been way more expensive than what she could afford. When she brought it home, she had had buyer's remorse, and dismissed it as not right for her. Still, it hung in her closet, all these years later. Why had she never given it away?

She took it out and laid it on the bed, eyed it critically. Not right for the old her. Perfect for the new her.

The dress was red as blood and had a low V on both the front and back, which meant she couldn't wear it with any bra that she owned.

It was the dress of a woman who was not filled with unreasonable fears.

Feeling ridiculously racy for the fact she had on no bra, she slipped the dress over her head, then looked at herself in her full-length mirror. She remembered why she had pur-

chased the dress, and it wasn't strictly because of the salesclerk gushing over it.

The dress gave Isabella a glimpse of who
she could be. It was as if it took her from
mouse to siren in the blink of an eye. She
looked confident and sexy and like a woman
who was uninhibited and knew how to have
fun and let go. It was the dress of a woman
who had the satisfying knowledge she could
have any man she wanted.

Isabella put makeup on the bump on her
head and then arranged her hair over it. She
dabbed mascara on her lashes and blush on
her cheeks. She glossed her lips and put on a
little spray of perfume.

She found her highest heels, and a tiny
clutch handbag, and a little silver bracelet.
Taking a deep breath, she marched out of her
room. Connor's bedroom door was closed.
Summoning all her courage, she knocked on
the door.

After a long moment, long enough for her
heart to pound in her throat as if it planned
to jump out of her, the door opened. He stood
there looking down at her. He was wet, still,
from the water from the broken shower spewing all over him, from helping her. Awareness
of him tingled along her spine.

She was so glad she had put on the red dress when Connor's mouth fell open before he snapped it shut. Something flashed in his eyes before he quickly veiled it. But even if she had led a sheltered life, Isabella knew desire when she saw it.

He folded his arms over his chest.

"My, my," he growled.

She tossed her head, pleased with the way his eyes followed the motion of her hair. "I'm going to a birthday party. I wanted to apologize before I left. I have never hit a person in my whole life. I'm deeply ashamed."

"Really?" he growled doubtfully.

"Really," she said, lifting her chin.

"That's kind of not the dress of someone who is deeply ashamed."

"The dress has nothing to do with this!"

"I think it does."

"Explain yourself."

He lifted a shoulder. "All right. I think you're a boiling cauldron of repressed passion."

"Maybe it's not repressed," she snapped.

His eyes went to her lips and stayed there long enough to make the point that they could find out how repressed or unrepressed she was right this second if she wanted. Her eyes skittered to his lips. She blinked first and looked away. When she looked back, his gaze was unflinching.

"In a dress like that, lots of people are going to want to find out, *is she, or isn't she?* You aren't going be lonely for very long at all."

Since the whole idea of putting on the dress had been to look passionate, why did she want to smack him again? And badly. She could tell this apology was premature. She had to grip her clutch extra tightly to keep her hand from flying free and hitting him across his handsome, smug face.

No, she didn't want to smack him. That wasn't the truth at all. The truth was exactly as he had said. She was a boiling cauldron of repressed passion, and she wanted to throw herself at Connor and let all that repressed passion boil out.

Isabella was absolutely appalled with herself. She took a step back from him and turned away. "Have a good evening, signor," she said formally, the prim little schoolteacher after all, a child playing dress-up in her red finery.

"Yeah. You, too."

She turned and walked away. And just

because she knew he was watching her, or maybe to prove to herself she wasn't just playing dress-up, she put a little extra swing in her step and felt the red dress swirl around her.

She glanced over her shoulder and caught him still watching her, his eyes narrowed with unconcealed masculine appreciation.

Surprisingly, given that unsettling encounter with Connor, Isabella did have a good evening. Sixteenth birthday parties for young women were a huge event in Monte Calanetti. It was a coming-of-age celebration, probably very much like a debutante ball in the southern US. The party signified the transition from being a child to being a woman.

While looking at the giggling young woman, Valerie, flushed with excitement in her finery, Isabella was struck by how extremely young and innocent she was. She was no more an adult that Isabella was an astronaut.

And yet Isabella had been sixteen herself when she had first declared her undying love for Giorgio. And how adult and sophisticated and sure of herself she had felt at that time. Now, watching this young woman, it seemed it would be laughable to make a lifelong declaration of love at that age, and then to feel bound by it.

The pensive thoughts did not last long, though. Isabella had been seated with some of her coworkers, and the talk turned to preparations for the spring fete and anticipation of the royal wedding being held in Monte Calanetti.

Then there was harmless gossip about who was getting married and divorced and who was burying parents. And, of course, in an Italian village, what was loved more than a pregnancy?

Nothing. But with each pregnancy revealed, Isabella felt happy and yet crushed, too. She did not think envy was an admirable emotion, and yet the thought of someone holding that beautiful, wiggling, warm bundle of life filled her with a terrible sense of longing for the life she did not have. And would probably never have. Not now.

"Have you heard? Marianna is pregnant."

Again Isabella's happiness for Marianna was laced with her own sense of loss. She listened halfheartedly as the circumstances around Marianna's pregnancy were placed under the microscope of the small, close-knit village. They were not ideal.

Italy was still mostly Catholic, and small

towns like Monte Calanetti were very traditional. A pregnancy without the benefit of marriage still raised eyebrows. There was some conjecture around the table about how Marianna's brothers, the staunchly conservative Angelo and Nico, might have reacted to news of a pregnancy.

After it had been discussed to death, it was all put aside and a decision was made.

"We will have to have a baby shower."

This was announced with a sigh of pure happiness and murmurs of delight from the other women. A baby in Italy was always seen as a blessing.

For some reason that made Isabella think of Connor talking about the abandonment of his mother by his father. Marianna's beau looked like the kind of man who would stand by her no matter what. Angelo and Nico, while they might rage and wring their hands, would never turn their backs on their own blood. Never.

Isabella wondered if that was the root of Connor wanting to protect the whole world— a little boy wanting to protect his mother. The thought made her heart ache for him. Not that she wanted to spoil this evening with one single thought about her houseguest!

Though Isabella was careful with the wine, some others were not, and the jokes became quite ribald and the laughter loud. The gathering was around a torch-lit courtyard, and after the dinner the tables were cleared away for dancing, and a live band came out.

The dress made Isabella feel different, less repressed and more carefree. To her astonishment, men she'd known for years were lining up to ask her to dance, and she soon felt as if she was flushed with as much excitement as the young Valerie.

It was after one in the morning before she realized how late it was.

"I have to work in the morning!"

She refused an offer to be walked home, and instead went down the darkened streets by herself. Partway home, she realized her feet ached from all the dancing, and she slipped off her shoes and went barefoot.

A little ways from her house, she saw a figure coming toward her. She knew from his size and the way he carried himself exactly who it was, and she felt her heart begin to race.

But his walk was different, purposeful, the strides long and hard, like a gladiator entering the arena, like a warrior entering the battlefield.

He stopped in front of her and gazed down at her. His eyes were flashing with cold anger.

"Where the hell have you been?"

"Scusi?"

"You heard me."

"I told you I was at a birthday party," she said.

"Well, I assumed a child's birthday party, and I thought it would be over at a decent time."

"What's it to you?" she snapped, angry at his high-handed manner, angry that he thought he could treat her like a child on the night she felt sexy and adult.

Her tone was louder than she intended. In fact, both their tones might have been louder than they thought. A light came on in a window above the street.

Connor stepped back from her, ran a hand through his hair and looked away. "You're waking the neighbors," he said, glancing up at that window.

"Me?" she said, unrepentant.

"Us," he conceded.

"Well, I have an excuse—boiling cauldron of repressed passion that I am, I am now shrieking like a fishwife in the streets. What's yours?"

"Good question," he said.

"You rescued me this afternoon. That does not put you in charge of my life!"

"You're right," Connor said. The anger had faded from his face. Instead, he looked faintly confused. Her own annoyance at him ebbed away a little bit.

"Are you out here looking for me?" she asked, astounded.

He could barely look at her, but he nodded.

What remained of her anger drained away. "But why?" She remembered thinking earlier tonight, with the news of Marianna's pregnancy, of the burden he had placed on himself of looking after the whole world. She remembered wondering if the first person he had felt protective of was his mother.

Almost against her will, something in her softened toward him.

"Hell, I started thinking about you bumping your head. It can be such a tricky injury. I should have checked more for signs of concussion."

"You were worried about me," she said. It was not a question.

"It's just that you'd had quite a bang on the

head, and you were dressed like that, and I started thinking you might not be making the best decisions."

"I'm thirty-three years old!"

"But you'd had a head injury. And you said you were lonely... I thought you might be..." His voice trailed away uncomfortably.

She looked at him silently. She should be insulted. He thought she might be what? Getting carried away with the first man who looked at her with avarice? But poor Connor looked tormented. His expression stole her indignation away from her.

"Vulnerable," he continued.

That was so true. She did feel very vulnerable. But it seemed he felt vulnerable, too.

"It's not that you wouldn't make good decisions under normal conditions," he said hastily. "But a bump on the head can cause confusion. Alter judgment slightly. I'm sorry. Am I making a fool of myself?"

"No," she said softly, "you are not. I am quite touched by your concern for me."

"I'm not sure it's rational," he said. "It's just that, unfortunately, I've just seen a lot of people get themselves in trouble before they know what's happened to them."

"I wasn't in trouble. But the party wasn't

for a child. Not really. For a sixteen-year-old. It's a big deal in Monte Calanetti. Almost like a wedding. A meal and dancing. The party could go on all night."

"I hate it when I act from emotion," he said gruffly.

"Do you?"

He stepped one step closer to her. He lifted her hair off her shoulder with his hand. "What are you doing to me?" he asked huskily. "I feel as if I'm not thinking straight."

"Ah."

"I find you very beautiful. It's hard for a man to think straight around that."

"It's just the dress," she said.

"No, Isabella, it's not."

"It's not?"

"There's something about you that makes me think with my heart instead of my head."

"Oh, dear," she said, and her tone was playfully mocking.

"Here's what I think," he said firmly, as if he had it all figured out.

"Yes?"

"I should take you on a date."

CHAPTER FIVE

ISABELLA STARED AT CONNOR. He should take her on a date? But was that his head or his heart talking? Because the way he said it, it was almost as though he hoped to get her out of his system.

"You should?" she asked.

"Sure. I mean, if you'd like to."

There was something very endearing about seeing this big, self-assured, superconfident Texan looking so unsure of himself.

"I'd like to," she said softly. "I'd like to, very much."

And then it seemed slightly and wonderfully ridiculous that they turned and walked home together.

Only it didn't seem ridiculous when his hand found hers.

It felt not as if she was going to go on a real date for the first time in her life, but as if she was coming home.

* * *

"I've gone and done something really stupid," Connor whispered into his phone.

"Huh? Who is this?"

"Justin, it's me."

"Connor?"

"Yeah."

"What the hell is going on?"

"There's this girl."

Something relaxed in Justin's tone. "This better be good—it's two o'clock in the morning here."

Connor contemplated that. Was there one rational thing left in him? No, that's why he was consulting his friend. That's what SEALs did when they were in a pickle, they relied on each other.

"She's not really a girl. A woman."

"Uh-huh?"

"I asked her out."

"That sounds like it's worthy of a two a.m. phone call."

"The thing is, I didn't really ask her out for me. I asked her out for her. She's a widow. She married really young. She's missed a lot. She's never been on a real date before."

Silence.

Connor sighed. "I'm the wrong guy for this, aren't I?"

Silence.

"I mean, I'm just the wrong guy to try and show her how it can be."

"How what can be?"

"You know."

"You'll have to spell it out for me. I'm having that two-o'clock-in-the-morning brain fart."

"How it can be, uh, when two people like each other. A lot."

"You mean falling in love?" Justin asked. He sounded wide-awake now.

"No!" Connor had to backtrack. He was sorry he had admitted liking her. A lot. His mission was one of altruism, and he wanted to make Justin understand that.

"I mean maybe falling in love," Connor said carefully, "just not with me. I just want to show her life can be fun. I want to show her she's missed something, and not to be afraid to embrace it. That it is not too late for her."

"From the embracer of all things romantic," Justin said wryly.

"You're not helping! I guess I want to show her what she should be looking for in a guy. Not me. I mean, I'm leaving. I'm here for the short term only. But if I could just give her an idea how a date should feel."

"Very altruistic."

"Are you being sarcastic?"

Justin sighed. "Okay. Ask me a specific question, and I will try to help you with it."

"What should I do with her on a date? I was thinking dinner and a movie."

"So, basically the same thing you've done on every single date you've ever been on?"

"Yes."

"Hmm."

"What does that mean?" Connor demanded. "I hate it when you say *hmm* like that."

"It just seems to me if you're trying to show her life is good, and trying to encourage her to embrace the great adventure, and trying to show her what a good date would feel like, you should put a bit more thought into it."

"I've been thinking of nothing else!"

"Just a sec." Connor could hear Justin talking to someone, the sound muffled as if he had stuck the phone under his pillow. Connor was pretty sure the other voice was feminine. He strained his ears. Justin came back on a moment later.

"Be original. A picnic in the moonlight. Something like that."

"That is the hokiest thing I've ever heard."

"Well, then, don't ask."

"Okay, I won't." And Connor contemplated the fact that Justin was with someone. Justin really was getting on with his life. It occurred to Connor that the wheelchair Justin used was holding Connor back more than it was his friend.

"Don't hang up, Connor. The red line is going off."

The red line. That was the dedicated line for emergencies for their company.

Justin came back on the phone. His voice was completely different, the sleep stripped from it. This voice, crisp, take-charge and take-no-prisoners, was a voice Connor recognized. He was a warrior now, and Connor shifted into that role easily, aware he was far more at ease with this than the places of the heart that he had very nearly gone to.

"How long would it take you to get back to Azerbaijan?"

Connor was already opening a different screen on his phone, looking up flights. "I could be in Baku in under six hours if I can make the connections."

"A vulture has landed. Go."

A vulture had landed. It was their code

for a bad guy, known to them. In a similar code, Justin and whoever was on the ground in Azerbaijan would text the details to Connor's phone as they had them. Connor was aware as he threw things in his bag that he felt a sense of purpose and mission. This was the world he moved in with absolute ease. This was where he belonged.

He scrawled a note for Isabella, sent a quick text to Nico and slipped out the door, back into the comfort of all that was familiar.

It was ironic just how safe danger made Connor Benson feel.

Isabella was aware, as soon as she woke up the next morning, that Connor was gone. She could feel his absence in the house, as if some energy that was necessary to life was gone.

She found his note on the kitchen table but was not comforted by it. Was it convenient that he was suddenly called away at the same time things were taking a turn between them? Was he deliberately cooling things off?

Isabella nursed the hope that he would call, and it increased her tension when he did not. He *was* cooling things off.

Still, she could not believe it was possible to miss Connor so much. In the short time he had been part of her life, his presence had made a big impact on her household without her really realizing it at the time. There was something about having a man in her house—even though they had mostly avoided each other—that made her feel safe. That in itself was not really rational—he had attacked her the very first day.

So, no, her acute sense of missing him had very little to do with a sense of safety. Maybe even the opposite. There was a sense that very *unsafe* things could unfold between them. And that made each day have a delicious sense of anticipation.

She looked at his note, over and over, trying to glean any emotion from it, trying to discern which way the compass was swinging. His handwriting was no surprise, strong and bold. The message was to the point: "Called away on business. Will pay for my room for days I am not here. Please hold for my return."

Given their middle-of-the-street conversation of the night before he had written that note—given his invitation to go on a date—it seemed very impersonal and businesslike. He had signed it only with his first name, no term of endearment.

What would she expect? *Love, Connor.* No, definitely not that. *Hugs?* That was laughable. How about *best wishes*? Or *can't wait to see you again*?

Despite all her misgivings, Isabella could feel herself anticipating his return like a child anticipating Christmas, even though she chided herself not to.

He had asked her on a date. If he followed through, she wondered what he had in mind. She felt excited about it, when really, that was the most unsafe thing of all.

Or maybe she really did not know the first thing about safety. Because she turned on the news one night, and it was focused on Azerbaijan. Normally, Isabella did not watch the news, and she would have flipped by the station. But tonight, she recalled that first morning Connor had said that was where he was coming from. Was that where his business had called him back to?

And indeed, the story was about an incident that had happened at the World Food Conference. Members of an unnamed private security organization had apprehended someone who had made threats against one of the delegates. Details were sketchy, and there was no footage. Had Connor's company been involved? Her gut said it had been.

When the story was over, Isabella shut off the TV, but she sat there until the room grew dark, thinking about what she had seen.

She was aware her stomach was in a knot. She was aware that *this* would be the reality of tangling your life with a man like Connor Benson.

Six days after he departed, a knock came on her front door. It was dinnertime, and Isabella was not sure who would come calling at that hour.

She swung open the door to see Connor standing there.

He looked so wondrously familiar. Her heart began to pound unreasonably. Her anxiety about the kind of work he did left her in a rush of warm relief to see him standing there, so obviously unharmed.

"Oh!" she said. She could feel herself blushing as she stepped back from the door. "You didn't have to knock. You live here."

He cocked his head at her, lifted a brow.

"I mean, you're a guest here. I want you to feel you can come and go as you please."

"I know that, but I also knew you didn't

know when I would be back. I didn't want to startle you. Again."

She regarded him. His face was deeply etched with exhaustion. But there was something else there, too. It was as she had suspected when she read his curt note—he had bought himself some time and now he seemed remote, as if they wanted different things. It was as if he had thought about that late-night meeting in the street and decided he wanted something different than what she wanted. He wanted them to be strangers. She wanted them to be friends.

Or more than friends?

Her anxieties were realized. Isabella could feel the excitement that had been building about his return leaving her like air hissing out of a pricked balloon.

"Come in," she said. "It's hot outside. Are you hungry?"

He hesitated. Isabella had the feeling they were not back at square one, they were somewhere even before square one. Was he going to pretend he had never even asked her on a date?

"Come eat," she said, more forcefully than she intended. She felt as if she did not want to give him room to retreat, physically, to his room, or emotionally, away from her.

She suspected it was because Connor was a soldier, and he responded to the command in her voice. He dropped his bag inside the door and followed her into the kitchen. He took a chair at the table, and she moved to get him some of the pasta she had made for her own dinner. Now, passing it to him, she could see even more clearly the exhaustion in the lines of his face. His mouth had a stern set to it, as if smiling was foreign to him.

She felt guilty. Whatever he had just come from, it had been hard, and it had taken a very obvious toll on him. What was she thinking, making this all about her?

"Where have you been?" she asked, lowering herself in the seat across from him.

"Just a job."

"Ah. Azerbaijan?"

He frowned at her.

"The World Food Conference?"

"The conference is over now. Everything went fine." He dug into the pasta like a starving man. It did her heart good to see him eat like that, even if he was doing it to avoid her.

"I saw something about it on television one

night. Was there some kind of threat made against some of the delegates?"

His voice was cool, it didn't invite probing. "Everything went fine," he repeated.

"Someone was apprehended."

"Really?"

"Really. By the private firm that looked after security for the event."

He lifted his eyebrows at her. *So what?*

"Were you in danger?" she asked him softly.

He lifted a shoulder. "Not particularly."

She knew then that he *had* been in danger, and that he shouldered the dangers of his job with the ease of long practice. This was not a man you could be timid with. This was not a man you could beg not to go to his world because it would soothe something in you. She found she had more courage than she ever would have believed. Because she felt proud of him, and in awe of his strength.

"Ah, Itus," she said. "Ever humble."

He looked up from his plate, lifted a brow at her. "What do you know about Itus?"

"I know in Greek mythology, he is the god of protection."

"It's just a name," he said. "My business partner, Justin, named the company. He picked that name. I am not a Greek mythology kind of guy."

"I wonder if your business partner was thinking of you when he chose that name."

Connor frowned, uninviting, but she went on anyway.

"Because Itus was very like you," she said quietly.

"Me?" He snorted, self-deprecating.

"Yes, you."

"In what way?" Connor had a bemused look on his face.

"He was a mortal boy, only seventeen when he was chosen to protect the god Apollo. He was given two swords, and he became so good with them that he beat the god Ares in a sword fight, though he would not boast about it. Apollo wanted to make him a god, and Zeus agreed, possibly because he did not want any more of his gods beaten in sword fights with mere mortals. Itus refused the honor. He did not feel he was worthy, but Apollo insisted and made him eat the food that would make him immortal."

Connor actually cast a wary glance down at his pasta.

"Then Apollo released him from his duties, and Itus now spends his days protecting the innocent from those who would do them harm."

"Look—" he set down his utensils, very deliberately "—Isabella, there is no use thinking there is anything the least romantic about me. Or what I do. It's hard, dirty, dangerous work—"

"You forgot lonely," she said quietly.

"—and it makes me a poor choice for a companion. No, not a poor choice. The worst choice. I should have never asked you out on a date. It was stupid and frivolous."

She felt the sharp bite of disappointment, but she was not totally unprepared for it. The crispness of his note had hinted this might be coming. At the same time, she could see it was the result of the events he had just come from that made something so simple as going on a date seem frivolous to him.

"I've decided," he said, his voice curt, "a date between us is out of the question. I mean, we are living together under the same roof for two more weeks. It's just way too awkward."

"I agree," she said soothingly.

That seemed to pull him up short. He regarded her suspiciously and then continued, "I mean, if I'm going to spend time with you,

I should make it count. I should teach you something useful."

She found herself gazing at his lips, thinking she had an idea or two what she'd like Connor Benson to teach her. "What would that be?"

"I should teach you how to swim."

"Instead of a date," she clarified.

He nodded vigorously. "It's not good to go through life with fears."

"Ah." It seemed ironic that he would say that when it was more than apparent he might have a fear or two about the date he had asked her on. She decided now might not be the best time to point that out to him.

"Once you know how to swim," Connor said seriously, "it gives you confidence and courage in dealing with all kinds of things that come up in life."

But not dates. Again, Isabella bit her tongue to keep herself from saying it out loud. So, her Itus did not want to date her, but he still wanted to protect her, or give her some tools to protect herself.

"Someday I believe you will have children," he continued sternly. "You can give them no greater gift than comfort in the water."

She could argue with him, of course. It seemed unlikely she would ever have children. But if she did, it seemed to Isabella there were all kinds of gifts parents gave their children, and that the greatest of those was love, not swimming lessons.

But he was in full retreat, and she had a feeling that the mention of the word *love* would probably push him right out her door and out of her life, so she bit her tongue again. It was probably good to learn this tongue-biting skill. You would need it a great deal around a man like him.

"I would be deeply appreciative if you would teach me how to swim," Isabella said.

He looked at her, wary of her demure tone.

She smiled back at him, though she had to bite her tongue, yet again, to keep from laughing out loud. She could so clearly see he was terrified of going on a date with her. His terror made her feel powerful and attractive and sexy. She had never really felt those things before. It was worth facing her own terror of the water dead-on.

A swimming lesson? He didn't know what he was letting himself in for. In fact, Connor Benson had no idea that he was teaching her already, all about the nature of confidence and courage.

"When should we start?" she asked, sweetly. "And where?"

"I'll arrange with Nico to use his pool," Connor said. "An hour, every afternoon from tomorrow, Monday to Friday, should give you the basics."

"I can learn to swim in five days?"

"Well, you won't be trying out for the Italian swim team, but you'll have some basic skills you can practice."

"Thank you," she said, lowering her eyes from his so he would not see the glee dancing in hers. When she looked back up, Connor was eyeing her suspiciously. Then he pushed back from the table and left the room.

"Things are improving between us," she said softly to herself. "I managed to feed him something before he ran away this time."

He probably hadn't considered that little detail when he was planning swimming lessons. No, Connor had probably not given a single thought to how hard it was going to be to run away from her in a swimming pool, especially since she had no love of the water. She'd be clinging to him like a barnacle to the bottom of a boat.

But there was another problem. Where, in a tiny place like Monte Calanetti, on such short notice, was she going to find the right bathing suit for this? Obviously she would have to make do with what she could find for tomorrow.

But he'd said it would take a week.

It was so much better than a date! A whole week.

She went into her office and shut the door. She flipped on her computer and typed the words she wanted into the search engine. Then she narrowed the search by putting in the necessary delivery dates.

By the time Isabella was done, she felt extremely naughty. The way she had felt in the red dress should have been fair warning to her, and to Connor, both.

Isabella Rossi *liked* feeling naughty.

As Connor was waiting in the water of Nico's beautiful pool, Isabella came through the back gate and gave him a quick wave before ducking into the cabana beside the pool.

He was pleased to note she looked particularly understated today in a longish skirt in a dull shade of beige and a baggy blouse in the same color. Her glossy hair was pulled back tightly, and she was carrying a large book bag that she was hugging to her chest. Really? She looked more like a nerdy student than the teacher.

He surveyed the pool while he waited for her. It was nestled in the garden grotto behind the house, and the pool had been made to look like a pond. Ferns trailed fronds in the water, and there was a small waterfall at one end of it.

Lovely as it was aesthetically, it was not really a pool for serious swimming, but it was large enough to do a few strokes, plus it had a deep end. It was about the furthest thing from the pools he had done SEAL training in, but it would do for an introduction to swimming basics.

Connor was feeling enormously pleased with himself. Teaching Isabella how to swim—instead of going on a date—had been a brainstorm. Swimming, after all, was useful. Tackling an irrational fear was useful. When he left this place, he would leave her with a skill that would be practical to her for her whole life. He would leave her with a sense of herself that was different than what it had been before. That sounded quite a bit better than leaving her with the heartache that a date promised.

She was staying here in this idyllic little village in Tuscany, and he was leaving, so what was the sense of exploring the sparks that were flying between them?

Isabella came out of the cabana. She had taken her hair out of the elastic when it would have been more sensible to leave it in. She had on an enormous poncho-like caftan that covered her from her head to her toes. It had hideous wide stripes in a crazy array of colors. It reminded him of pictures he had seen of what people wore to music festivals in the '60s.

When she stood on the deck he was at eye level with her feet. Her toenails were painted lime green, and as odd a choice as that was, he had to admit it was adorable, and a little less nerdy than the rest of her ensemble.

"What's that thing?" he asked her. He noticed that her face had been scrubbed free of makeup, probably in preparation for her swim.

"What thing?"

"That thing you're wearing."

She looked down at herself. "Oh. My swim cover."

He had to bite back a smile. She had to wear a swim cover to get from the cabana to the pool? The walk might have been twenty yards.

"Well, how about if you take it off and get in the water."

She hesitated. He could see the pulse beating in her throat. She looked past him at the water and gulped.

"Believe me, you can't swim with it on."

"Oh," she said, as if he was breaking world news to her. Isabella reached for the zipper, and closed her eyes. Because she was afraid of the water? Or was she sweetly shy about being seen in her swimming suit?

She bent over to get the zipper undone. Her swim cover was still doing its job. Covering. The zipper stuck partway down, and she tugged and tugged, but nothing happened. Suddenly, in frustration, she gave up on the zipper and pulled the caftan from her shoulders. As she was freed from the bulky covering, it slid down and settled in a lump at her waist.

Connor stared helplessly.

Her eyes locked on his. He looked away, focusing on those little green toenails, not sure he wanted her to see what he was thinking.

She pushed the caftan away from her waist and it floated to the ground, at his eye level, creating a puddle that looked like a burlap bag around her little monster-toed feet.

He was left looking at the length of her lovely legs. Then she stepped out of the fabric puddle and kicked the covering aside.

Connor reminded himself he had seen her in a transparent shower curtain. And a red dress that had made his mouth go dry. Whatever this was, it could not be any worse than that. Isabella was a practical schoolteacher. She would know how to pick a good bathing suit.

Having thus reassured himself, Connor cocked his head upward to see more than her feet and her legs. His mouth fell open. He gulped. He snapped his mouth shut so that the practical schoolteacher would not guess how much she was rattling his world.

A swimming lesson? Whose dumb idea had this been?

She was wearing one of the tiniest swimsuits he had ever seen, if you could call that scrap of fabric—three scraps of fabric—a swimsuit. Isabella was wearing a string bikini in an amazing shade of lime green that made her skin look as golden as the sand at a beach in New Zealand, Kaiteriteri, that he had visited once. Her dark hair spilled over that golden expanse of skin, shiny and beautiful.

"Is something wrong?" she asked. Her tone was all innocence, but he wasn't fooled. No woman put on a bathing suit like that without knowing exactly what she was doing!

Suck it up, he ordered himself. He'd seen her in a shower curtain. Nothing could be worse than that. Except this was worse than that. It was worse, even, than the red dress.

Isabella Rossi, village schoolteacher, nerdy girl, was smoking hot!

"Wrong?" he choked out, not willing to give her the victory. "What could possibly be wrong?"

"I don't know. You have a look on your face."

"A look on my face?" he demanded.

"Mmm. Like you've been smacked with a frozen fish."

He wiped whatever look he had on his face off. He felt as though he'd been smacked, all right, and not with a frozen fish. Smacked with awareness of her. He had the ugly feeling she wasn't as innocent as she appeared. In fact, Connor had the ugly feeling that she might be toying with him.

He forced himself to find his voice. It had to be addressed. "You really should have left your hair up."

"Oh? Why's that?"

What was he doing talking about her hair? He needed to tell her the bathing suit wasn't going to work. At all. "You don't want to get it in your face."

"I'm not planning on getting my face wet."

"You have to get your face wet. To swim."

She didn't look the least convinced. She dismissed him with a little wave of her hand. "Oh, well, maybe next time I'll get my face wet."

Address it, he ordered himself. "Uh, that bathing suit—"

"Yes?" Her voice was husky.

"—is really nice."

Now, *that* he had not meant to say. At all. Isabella was beaming at him.

"—but, it isn't, er, really made for swimming."

Unless he was mistaken, and he was pretty sure he was not, the little minx was lapping up his discomfort.

"It's called a bathing suit," she said stubbornly.

"Maybe it's for *sun*bathing. I mean, if you were to dive in the water with that thing…"

His voice trailed away.

"I'm not planning on diving today, either," she informed him primly.

Wait a minute. Who was in charge here? He suspected, in that bathing suit, she was. "Well, I wasn't planning on that, either, but—"

"The bathing suit will have to suffice," she said. The schoolteacher voice was very at odds with the drop-dead gorgeous woman standing in front of him. "Selection—"

Seduction? No, no, she'd said *selection*, not *seduction*.

"—is very limited in Monte Calanetti at this time of year. I ordered some other things on the internet. They should arrive soon."

How soon was soon, he wanted to demand. Maybe they could postpone.

"I'm sure it will be fine," Isabella said, "You already said it's not as if I'm training for the national swim team."

She had him there. He wanted to teach her enough to hold her own if she fell out of a boat. Or in the river. Or got carried away unexpectedly by a current. He wanted to teach her enough that being around water did not make that pulse go crazy in her throat, like a rabbit being chased by dogs. The way it was now.

Was that because she was about to get wet? Or was it because she was trying out her bold new self on him?

Connor considered, again, postponing. He glanced at her face. A tiny little smile was playing across her lips before she doused it. She *was* toying with him!

"Get in the water," he snapped. The sooner she was covered up with anything, including water, the better. If the bathing suit fell off, or melted, they'd deal with that when it happened. Just as they had dealt with the shower catastrophe.

But really, how much could one man take?

Isabella stuck her toe in and yanked it back out. She made a face. She hugged herself, either not as confident in the skimpy suit as she wanted him to believe or suddenly aware that she was tackling something she was afraid of.

"I can't just jump in," she decided.

She could sit on the edge of the pool, reach out and put her hands around his neck... Connor gave himself a shake. This was going to be quite hard enough! "There are stairs at that end."

She looked where he was pointing and saw the stairs entering the pool at the shallow end. She eyed her dropped caftan for a second, as if she was considering putting it back on for the short walk to the stairs. Or putting it back on and fleeing.

Instead, she tilted her chin up and went over there, wiggling her hips self-consciously the whole way. It gave Connor plenty of opportunity to study how much of her was not covered by those skimpy green scraps of fabric. It also gave him plenty of opportunity to set his face into a mask of indifference.

At the top of the stairs, she repeated the put-one-toe-in-and-withdraw-it procedure. Still in the water, he slogged his way over to that end of the pool and stood close to the bottom of the stairs.

"At this rate we are still going to be here tomorrow," he groused out loud, instead of saying what he really wanted, which was *get in the water, dammit.*

She held up a hand, a very Italian gesture that warned him not to hurry her, and then Isabella proceeded to get into the water with painful slowness.

CHAPTER SIX

As Connor watched, Isabella got on the first stair leading into the pool. She was acting as if the world was tilting and her life depended on her hanging on to the handrail.

The world was tilting, and Connor felt as if his life depended on her getting in the water. With the water at her ankles, she paused there, allowing him to wallow in the full impact of that bathing suit. Was that a piercing, right below her belly button? Was his jaw clenched?

"The easiest way is just to jump in," he told her. Yes, definitely clenched. He deliberately relaxed it.

"Never let it be said I'm easy."

He contemplated her. Her command of English and all its nuances and slang was not good enough for her to have meant that the way it sounded. Though the beautiful young widow was probably about the furthest thing from easy that he had ever met.

She went down one more step. Now she was up to her knees. She had both hands on the handrail. Her knuckles were white.

"I thought the water would be warmer," she said.

"It's perfect." His jaw was clenching again.

She wrinkled her nose, letting him know their ideas of perfect were different, which would be a very good thing for him to keep in mind, because a bathing suit like that made a man think he could make anything work out, even against impossible odds.

And the odds were impossible. Everything about them was different. He was large, she was tiny. He was powerful, she was fragile. He was cynical, she was innocent. They were culturally a million miles apart. He's seen colleagues fall for the seemingly exotic girls of foreign lands. It never worked.

He tried to hold those thoughts as, finally, Isabella was at the bottom of the steps, up to her cute little belly button in water. It was a little dark mole under her belly button, not a piercing. He was not sure which was sexier.

Isabella was still holding onto the handrail as if her life depended on it. He tried to remember why he had thought getting her in the water would be easier on him. It was not.

"Let go of the handrail and walk over to me," he said.

"Not yet." Her voice had a little quaver to it.

And that changed everything. Because it reminded him this wasn't about him. It wasn't about recalculating impossible odds. It was about her, giving her a few tools to deal with the harsh realities of life. And he could not let her scanty little bathing suit distract him from that. That's one of the things he was trained to do. Sift through information very quickly, ignore the distractions, focus on the mission.

So he crossed the distance that remained between them and pried her hand, ever so gently, off the handrail. He placed himself right in front of her and held out his other hand. She hesitated and then placed her hand in his.

Their hands joined as they faced each other, they were like two dance partners who had never danced together sizing each other up. It occurred to him this was going to be like no swimming lesson he had ever given before.

"Don't even look at the water," he said softly. "Just look at me."

Her eyes fastened on his face as if she was

drowning and he was the lifeline. Her gaze was as disconcerting as the bikini. Maybe more so. It made the mission waver a little more.

"See?" he said, forcing himself to speak, keeping his voice soft, and taking a step back, "No danger. No crocodiles. No chance of falling over a ledge. No current to sweep you away."

No danger. Ha-ha. Her hand, small but strong in his, felt like one of the gravest dangers he had ever encountered. Had he really thought getting her in the water was going to be better than watching her on the deck?

Now, added to his physical awareness of her hands in his, she was so close to him he could smell that spicy perfume that was hers and hers alone. It felt as if he was being swept away by the absolute trust in her eyes fastened on his, the way she was holding his hands. She took her first tiny step through the water toward him.

He backed up. She took one more. He backed up two. And then they were doing a slow waltz through the water. He was careful to stay in the shallows, even though it wasn't nearly deep enough to help him deal with the worst of the distractions. Was that tiny bathing suit top sliding sideways just a touch?

Connor repeated his command to himself.

Suck it up.

"See?" he said softly. "It's not so bad, is it? Just stay in the moment. Don't think one thought about what could happen."

She actually closed her eyes. A tiny smile touched her lips. He ordered himself not to look at her lips and definitely not to think about what could happen. Connor felt the purity of the moment—water on his skin, her hair shining in the sun, her small hands in his, the rapturous look on her face—seducing him.

Somehow, he'd had this utterly foolish idea that he was going to pretend she was a raw recruit and be able to keep professional distance from her as he taught her the basics of swimming. He was not sure how he had deluded himself. He had never had that much imagination. He'd always prided himself on being such a realist.

"The water does feel amazing on my skin," she breathed. Her eyes remained closed in wonder.

Connor cleared his throat. "So now you've seen the water in this end of the swimming pool holds no danger to you," he said, trying desperately to stick to the business at hand

and not think one single thought about her skin. "So, let's try the next step."

Her eyes flew open and that pulse in her throat picked up tempo. "What is the next step?"

"I'd like you to learn the water will support you. Human beings are buoyant. They float."

She looked doubtful about that—the pulse in her throat went crazy.

"Isabella, you will float."

"I'm scared."

"I know."

His life's work had presented him with this situation, again and again. He'd had plenty of encounters with people, civilians, who found themselves in difficult situations. Families who, through no fault of their own, found themselves in war zones. Hostages, in the wrong place at the wrong time, who didn't know the rule book, who had spent their entire lives blissfully oblivious to the fact there was a rule book.

Connor had led people from burning buildings, evacuated the terrified, navigated the fear of others in a thousand different ways. He'd dealt with people who were scared. He did it all the time.

He excelled at this: at infusing his abundance of confidence and calm into panicky people through his voice and his actions.

It felt different this time, way too personal, as if that enemy called fear was hovering at the edges of his own awareness. But that was his fault, not hers, bikini notwithstanding. He took a deep breath, gathered himself, formed a plan.

"I'm going to stand beside you," he said quietly, "with my hands like this. You are going to lie down in the water, on your back, and let my hands support you."

"Oh, God," she said in Italian. "I don't think I can. Could we just walk around some more? I was getting the hang of that. Walking in water. I think it's biblical."

"I think that may be walking *on* water."

"It's good enough for me. For today."

"Swimming lessons, heavy emphasis on the swimming."

"My hair isn't right. And the bathing suit won't work. You already said that."

"We'll figure it out. Together."

Together. He did not excel at figuring things out *together*. It had been his greatest weakness with the SEALs. He was not a good team player. He had a tendency to go maverick. The last time he had done it, against orders, Justin had followed him…

"Are you all right?" Her hand, wet, warm, was on his cheek.

He shook his head. How was it she could see what no one else ever saw? "Yeah. I'm fine."

She didn't move her hand. He didn't move it, either. He had to stop this craziness. He shook his head again, trying to be all business. But droplets of water flew off his hair and rained down on her face, emphasizing the compassion there.

"Lie down in the water." His voice had a snap to it, like a flag caught in the wind.

Isabella's hand dropped to her side, but Connor could feel the warmth of it on his face as if it still rested there.

"No, I—" She twisted and looked at the stairs.

"Trust me," he said in *that* voice, firm, the voice of a man who was used to being in charge of everything, including the safety of others.

She dragged her eyes back from the staircase and looked at him for a long moment. Her eyes, with the water reflecting in them, looked more green than gold.

"Okay," she whispered.

"So just lean back," he coaxed her.

She leaned back an inch.

"Maybe a little more."

She leaned back another inch, so stiff-spined she looked like a tree bending over. He sighed and moved into her swiftly, before she could guess what he was going to do. Maybe he didn't even know what he was going to do himself until he had done it.

He scooped Isabella up and held her against his chest.

"Oh," she sighed with surprise. She would have weighed about as much as a feather under normal circumstances. With the water taking most of her weight, it was like holding a puff of air.

Except that her skin was warm and sensual, like silk. She blinked up at him and then twined her arms around his neck.

What part of the Swimming 101 manual was this in? he demanded of himself. He pried her fingers from around his neck and put her away from his chest, supporting her body on his hands, at right angles from his own.

"Okay," he said. His voice was faintly hoarse, not completely his talking-a-hostage-away-from-the-bad-guy voice. "Just relax.

That's it. Now straighten out your legs. I've got you."

Tentatively, she did as he asked, her forehead wrinkled with anxiety as she gave herself over to the water. Her hair floated out in the water around her face, like dark silk ribbons. The small of her back was resting securely on his hands. Her skin was warmer than the water, and he felt a primal awareness of her that he did not want to feel.

At all.

"You're a bit tense," he told her. He heard the tension in his own voice and took a deep, steadying breath. "Relax. I won't bite."

"Yes," she said. "So you've said."

"Focus on your breathing. Put your hands on your tummy—no, you don't need them, I've got you—and breathe until you feel your tummy rising instead of your chest."

Shoot. Did he have to mention her chest just as his voice was returning to normal?

"This is quite amazing," she said after a moment.

"Amazing," he agreed. His jaw was starting to hurt from clenching his teeth so tightly. "So, just try moving your legs a bit. Kick."

She did a little kick.

"Very good," he encouraged her. "Harder, both of them."

She kicked tentatively. And then harder. The splash hit him in the face, which seemed to motivate more strenuous kicking on her part. She giggled.

That giggle helped him turn a page. Connor pretended to be worried about getting wet, ducking the worst of the splash while never letting her go. She giggled some more.

"Now straighten your legs out. Think of a pair of scissors opening and closing and kick like that. That's perfect. That's why it's called a scissor kick. Now, instead of just standing here, I'm going to let the kick propel you. I'll move with you, though. You see how it works? Your legs are amazingly strong."

What he meant was that everyone's legs were amazingly strong, that this particular movement used the gluteus maximus, the largest muscle in the human body, but he didn't clarify, since she looked so pleased. And there was no denying her legs were amazing!

He supported her and guided her until she had kicked around the pool in a large circle.

"Now," he said, "my hands are still here,

but I'm moving them away from you, so you can see it's the water supporting you, not me."

"No."

"Yes."

She glared up at him.

"Don't be nervous. The water's only three feet deep here. You can stand up at any time. Just relax. I'm going to—"

"No! Don't let go of me. I'm not ready."

He'd heard it again and again, looking into the eyes of a terrified civilian who was being asked to do something that required more of them than had ever been required before.

"Yes, you are," he said, "you are ready."

Slowly, he slid his hands out from underneath her. Her eyes grew wide, and then she got nervous, and her body folded at the center, legs and head going up, abdomen and torso going down, under the water.

"Ahh," she yelped.

His hands were floating inches below her, and so he supported her again, very quickly.

"Try and keep your body stiff."

"I thought I was supposed to relax!"

"Well, relaxed stiffness."

"There is no such thing."

"Maybe not in Italian. There is in English." He managed to say it with a straight face.

She smiled in spite of herself, and then he let her go, and she tried again. Again, she got nervous and began to fold; again he used his hands to steady her. The third time, she got it. She kicked on her own and he shadowed her.

"Am I swimming?" she demanded. "Am I swimming all by myself?"

He smiled at her enthusiasm, and she seemed to realize she was swimming, unaided, on her back. The realization ruined it, of course. This time he wasn't quite quick enough, and her head went under the water. She came up sputtering, her hair spilling rivulets of water down her golden skin. She grabbed for him and clung to him.

He realized he was enjoying that way too much and put her away from his chest, though he allowed her to hang on to his forearms.

"That wasn't so bad, was it?" he asked her.

She shook water from her hair. "No," she said, surprised and then delighted. "No, it was fine. I just held my breath when I went under."

There was a moment when people reached deep inside and found out who they really were that was awe-inspiring. It could happen as you sneaked them across a border or pushed them out of a plane, or it happened in those moments, large and small, when people required just a tiny bit more of themselves.

And so it could happen just like this, a woman in a swimming pool on a warm spring day when everything seemed suddenly infused with a light that was not the sun.

It was always an amazing thing to be a part of this moment. She was grinning ear to ear, which increased Connor's sensation of basking in the light. He had to force himself to move away from that moment and back on task.

"And that brings us to part two," Connor said. "For some reason, people have a natural aversion to getting their faces wet."

"I told you not today," she said. The grin disappeared.

"Let's just ride this wave of discovery," he suggested.

For a moment, she looked as if she intended to argue, but then, reluctantly, she smiled again. "All right. Let's ride this wave."

Both of them had said it—let's. Let *us*. Us. A duo. A team. Sheesh.

"So, before you dunk again, we're going to work on getting your face wet," Connor said. There it was again, slipping off his tongue naturally. *We.* "Lie on my hands again, this time on your stomach."

She flopped down on her stomach, and he supported her, his hands on the firm flesh of her belly. "Good. Now put your face in the water and blow air out of your mouth. Make bubbles. The more the better. Think of yourself as a motorboat."

Whatever reservations she might have had up until this point now disappeared. Isabella gave herself over to learning to swim with unreserved enthusiasm. With Connor supporting her stomach, she blew bubbles and then they added a scissor kick. She managed a few kicks without any support before she went under and came up laughing.

Isabella laughing.

Isabella soaking wet, in the world's skimpiest bathing suit, laughing.

It was probably one of the most dangerous moments of Connor's entire life, and he had had a life fraught with danger.

It wasn't dangerous because she was so beautiful, or even because she had lost her self-consciousness and she was so sexy in her teeny bathing suit. It wasn't dangerous because she was finding her inner resources of courage and strength.

No, what made the moment beautiful was her joy. What made the moment astounding was the serious expression gone from her face and the sorrow completely erased from her eyes. No matter what the danger to himself, Connor was glad he had given her this moment.

"I think that's probably enough for today," he said gruffly. "We'll start some basic arm work tomorrow, moving toward a front crawl. And we'll do work on your legs with a kickboard. By the end of the week, you'll be swimming across this pool by yourself."

"Really?"

"You are a complete natural."

"I am?" she asked, so pleased.

"Absolutely."

"What an amazing afternoon." She cocked her head at him. "What do the American teenagers say? Awesome!"

She was standing facing him. She leaned a bit closer. He had plenty of time to move away from her. But somehow he didn't, frozen to the spot, like a deer in headlights, not able to back away from where *awesome* could take them.

She stood on tippy toes. Her body, slippery and lithe, came in contact with his in a far different way than it had when he was using his arms to buoy her up in the water. She kissed him, a tiny brushing of their lips.

He, of all people, knew how little time it took to change everything. A millisecond. The time for a bullet to find its way from rifle to target, the time for tires to crunch across the trigger device on an explosive, the time for a school to go from rooms of laughing children to completely engulfed in flames. He, of all people, knew how quickly everything could change.

But maybe he hadn't known this: as quickly as you could be sucked into darkness and everything could shatter around you, just as quickly you could be thrust toward the light, propelled into a world that promised love was stronger.

Love? He felt furious with himself, and not too happy with Isabella, either. But then she was backed away from him, still laughing, that delightful, carefree, water-over-rocks laughter, as if she had no awareness at all how badly she had just disrupted his well-ordered world.

"Thank you, Connor. I can't wait for tomorrow."

And then she walked away from him,

through the water, by herself, the woman she had been an hour ago—clinging to the handrail and then to him—gone forever.

Isabella got out of the pool without the benefit of the stairs. She put her hands on the deck and levered herself out, wiggling her bottom at him in the process. And then, free of the pool, she gathered up that voluminous caftan but didn't put it on. She scampered across the deck to the cabana, not once looking back.

Thank goodness she did not look back. Because she would have seen him, still standing in the water, stunned by the power of that one tiny little brush of lips. To change everything.

The man he had been an hour ago might have been gone forever, too. Because the thing about a kiss like that? It opened a door. It opened a door that was pretty darned difficult to wrestle shut again once it had been opened. It changed everything in subtle ways.

Connor sucked in a deep breath. He said a word under his breath that he would never say in Isabella's presence. He dived under the surface of the water. His momentum carried him to one end of the pool. Though there was hardly room to get going, he began to do furious laps, butterfly stroke.

But by the time Isabella emerged from the cabana, he was aware that swimming had not defused what he was feeling. Even that most challenging stroke did not begin to burn off the fire that brush of her lips against his had stoked within him.

CHAPTER SEVEN

ISABELLA CONTEMPLATED THE fact that she had kissed Connor Benson. Really, as far as kisses went, it had been nothing. A peck. A thank-you.

But even in Italy, where people were passionate, a thank-you kiss might normally be placed on the cheek, not the lips.

Connor's lips looked so firm. And yet, giving under the pressure of hers, they had felt soft and pliable. His lips had tasted of something, but she wasn't sure what. It had been pure, like holding out your tongue to catch raindrops.

Heaven. That's what they had tasted of. The problem was, after tasting something like that, a person could spend her life in pursuit of it. It had really been a foolish thing to do, reckless, especially with them living under her roof together.

But in that moment, after the lesson, she had just felt so bold, so ready to do just as he suggested, to ride the wave of discovery instead of fighting it. It had been wonderful tackling the water, doing something she had always been afraid of. It had made her feel free in a way she never had before.

From the moment she had chosen that bathing suit over the far more conservative ones available, even with the limited selection in Monte Calanetti at this time of year, Isabella had felt she was saying yes to life.

The swimming lesson itself had made her feel so alive and so bold and as if the world and this day were plump with possibilities instead of just one day following the next, safe and routine.

Isabella came out of the cabana and saw that Connor was swimming like a man possessed. The stroke he was using was amazing, his powerful arms and shoulders lifting his torso and propelling him out of the water as if he had been shot out of a cannon.

He noticed her, she was not sure how, and he stopped and stood up. He folded his arms over the lines of his chest. Her awareness of him rippled through her like a current that could sweep her away.

"I forgot to tell you, I found another place to stay," he said.

She knew instantly he was lying. He hadn't found another place to stay. He had tasted the reckless danger, too, as soon as her lips had touched his, and decided to find different accommodations.

He was acknowledging something was going on between them. Something more powerful than he could control. And even though he had told her to ride the wave of discovery, he was not prepared to do that himself.

She held her breath. Was he going to cancel swimming?

"I'll see you tomorrow. And I'll pay you for your place for the agreed dates." he said. He dived back under the water before she could let him know she was not going to help him assuage his guilt by allowing him to pay her for a room he wasn't going to occupy.

Isabella had never really felt this before: an acute awareness of her feminine power.

She walked home by herself, aware that the buoyancy of the water seemed to have infused her. Even though Connor had said he was moving out, her steps were light, and she felt as if she was walking on air.

She got home to discover a parcel had been delivered. It was one of the bathing suits she had ordered online, from Milan. She was pleased it had been delivered so quickly, that overnight delivery had meant just that.

And she was even more pleased when she opened the parcel and slipped the fabric from the tissue paper. So tiny! How could it possibly have cost so much money? Still, she hugged the scraps of fabric to her and went to try the new suit on. It was no more a *swim*suit than the lime-green bikini today had been.

But she had given herself permission, with that first bold choice of a bathing suit, to start exploring a different side of herself. More feminine. More sexy. Deeply alive within her own body. Deeply appreciative of herself as a woman, and of the power that came with acknowledging this new side of herself.

Isabella was choosing the bathing suits of a woman who wanted a man to be very aware she was a woman. Not to just tease him, but to let him know he was not going to be able to shunt her aside so easily, just because he'd switched from a date to swimming lessons.

She thought of the way Connor had been swimming when she left Nico's garden area— like a man possessed, or at the very least, like a man trying to clear his head—and allowed herself the satisfied chuckle of someone who had succeeded beyond their wildest dreams.

Still, when she heard him come in later, pack his bags and leave, she avoided him. Already her house felt empty without him. If she went and saw him, she was not at all certain she could trust herself not to beg him to stay.

She would not beg him to stay, but she was not above making him sorry he had left.

The next day at the pool, she wore the same oversize caftan out onto the deck. Connor was in the pool tossing a blue flutter board into the air and catching it, pretending he'd barely registered her arrival.

But when she dropped the caftan, he registered her arrival—he missed his catch on the kickboard.

If it was possible, her new bathing suit, black and shiny, was even skimpier than the one she had worn yesterday. She really took her time getting into the water, savoring the scowl on his face.

When she reached the bottom stair, he shoved the kickboard at her and snapped some instructions.

"Aren't you even going to say hello?" she asked, petulant.

"Hello," he snapped.

"Your new accommodations must not be very nice."

"What would make you say that?"

"You seem like you haven't slept well or something. You have grumpy lines." She touched the sides of her own mouth to show him where. He stared at her mouth. His grumpy lines deepened.

"We're going to work on your kick today." And so they did. There was a lot less touching this second day of instruction. It was shameful how disappointed she was by that. He announced the session was over from the opposite end of the pool. Isabella was fairly certain this was to discourage thank-you kisses.

Though, even without the kiss, his swimming seemed even more furious when she left than it had the day before.

The third day, another bathing suit had arrived. It was not a bikini. It was a leopard-patterned one-piece with a plunging neckline and the legs cut very high. It was so racy— and not the competitive swimming kind of racy—that Isabella actually debated not wearing it at all.

But she was so glad she had when they sat side by side on the pool deck, legs dangling in the water for lesson number three. His mouth set in a grim line, Connor demonstrated the arm movements for the front crawl. Really? Him showing off his arm muscles like that was no more fair than her showing off in her bikini!

They ended the lesson in the water. With him at her side she managed to swim across the width of the shallow end of the pool, once on her back and then once on her front.

The only reason he touched her at all was because she swallowed some water and came up choking. He slammed her on the back a few times before ordering her back to work.

When she emerged from the cabana, she noticed that Connor was churning up enough water to create a tidal wave.

The fourth day, not wanting it to be too obvious she was enjoying driving him crazy, she put the lime-green bikini from the first day back on. He got her into the deep end. He taught her to tread water, arms doing huge swooping circles, legs bicycling.

"You don't work hard at it," he warned her. "You relax. It's something you should be able to do for a long, long time."

And then he made her do it for half an hour, treading water right beside her without ever touching her. Once again, when she left he was covering the pool in length-eating strokes.

The fifth day, she arrived at the pool in her newest bathing suit. It was too bad he'd left her house and she'd refused his money. It would have helped her afford all these suits.

This one was a simple black one-piece, a tank style. The most suitable for swimming, it made the light come on in his eyes just as the others had done.

"Today," he announced, "we'll do a quick review of everything we have learned, and then we're done."

Done. Isabella thought of that. No more seeing him every day, unless she caught glimpses of him in the village, going about his business. Her life would be as empty as her house.

And then the wedding would come and go, and he would be gone from Monte Calanetti for good. Forever.

She got in the water and stood at the bottom of the stairs.

"Don't stand there gripping the rail like that," he snapped. "You've come farther than that."

The tone! As bossy as if she was some

green recruit he had authority over. A beach ball, rolling around on the deck, pushed by the wind, plopped in the water beside her. On an impulse, she picked it up and hurled it at his head.

He caught it easily and squinted at her. For a moment she thought he was going to ignore her protest of his high-handed ways. But then he tossed the ball high in the air and spiked it at her. She swiveled out of the way with a little squeal. The ball missed her, and then she grabbed it. She threw. He dived under the water.

Connor resurfaced and grabbed the ball. He threw it hard. She, who a week ago had been afraid to get her face wet, ducked under the water. She came up and grabbed the ball. He was swimming away from her. She waded in after him, threw the ball when he stopped. It bounced off his head.

"Ha-ha, one for me," she cried.

He grabbed the ball and tossed it. It hit her arm. "Even. One for me, too." He swam right up to her, his powerful strokes bringing him to her in a breath. He grabbed the ball and let her have it from close range. "Two for me."

"Oh!"

Just like that, all the tension that had been

building between them for a week dissolved into laughter. They were playing. The last lesson was forgotten, and they were like children chasing each other around the pool, shrieking and laughing and calling taunts at each other.

And then she missed a throw and the ball bounced onto the deck. Neither of them bothered to get it, and now they were just playing tag without the ball between them. The air filled with their hoots of laughter. She tagged him with a shove and swam away. He came after her hard and splashed her, then tagged her and was off. She knew she couldn't possibly catch him, and so he was letting her shove him and splash him.

An hour went by. They were breathless, the air shimmering with their awareness of each other.

Reluctant for it ever to end, Isabella finally gave in first and hauled herself up on the deck and lay there on her tummy, panting, exhausted. A shadow passed over her. He was standing above her.

Isabella was aware she was holding her breath. He had moved out of her house to avoid her. But then, after a moment, he lowered himself to the deck, on his stomach, right beside her. He wasn't touching her, but he was so close she could feel a wave of warmth coming off the outer part of his arm.

He closed his eyes, and she unabashedly studied him. She could see how the water was beading on his skin, droplets tangled in his eyelashes, sunlight turning them to diamonds. She could see the smooth perfection of his skin, the lines of his muscles, the swimmer's broadness of his shoulders and back.

She had never, ever been more aware of another human being than she was of Connor, lying beside her. She sighed with something that sounded very much like surrender, and closed her eyes.

Lying there on the pool deck beside Isabella, Connor felt as if the whole world came to a standstill. When danger was near, he always felt this—his senses heightened until they were almost painful. And he felt it again right now, as he had never felt it before.

He could feel the gentle Tuscan sun on his back and the heat rising up through the pool deck and warming every cell of his skin. He could hear the birds singing, but more, he could separate their songs, so he could hear each one individually. She sighed—a contented sound like a kitten's mew—and he could feel the puff of air from that sigh touch his lips, as life-altering as her kiss had been.

He could smell the flowers that bloomed in abundance around the pool, the faint tang of chlorine and most of all Isabella. The spicy scent had been washed away and replaced by an aroma that was dizzying in its feminine purity.

He had only one sense left to explore. He opened his eyes and gazed at Isabella stretched out on the pool deck. Her hair hung thick and wet and luxurious down the narrowness of her back. Her black bathing suit clung to her like a second skin, caressing the curve of her back and the swell of her firm buttock. Her skin was as flawless as porcelain. The roundness of her cheek was pressed into the deck, and her lashes were so thick and long they cast a faint shadow there. Her lips had not a hint of lipstick on them, and yet they naturally called to him, full and plump and sensuous.

As if she sensed him studying her, she opened her eyes. He unabashedly threw himself into the color of them—it felt as if he was swimming in cool pools of sun-filtered greens and golds and browns.

A few days ago, he had gone to the chapel at

the palazzo. It had been strictly work. If he was a bad guy, where would he hide? What were the weak places both in the chapel and around it? He'd taken some pictures and made some notes of the exterior and then moved inside.

Logan Cascini, the project manager for the whole restoration, had come up to him. Connor had been touching base with Logan on and off since he arrived, and there was an affinity between the two men.

"You have to see what has complicated my life today," Logan had said wryly.

"That's gotta be a woman," Connor had muttered.

"That sounds like the voice of experience," Logan said, raising a quizzical eyebrow.

"Show me your complication," Connor said, not following Logan's implied invitation to elaborate.

"This is the final wall we're working on. We're just pulling off that old wood paneling."

Connor followed Logan over to a side wall of the church. The workmen were absolutely silent, their normal chatter gone.

As they uncovered it, Connor, who considered himself no kind of art lover, had stood there, frozen by the beauty of what he was seeing revealed.

"It's a fresco," Logan supplied, "probably centuries old, and probably by one of the lesser Renaissance painters."

"I've never seen anything so beautiful," Connor said when he could find his voice. The fresco was the Madonna and child. The expression on the Madonna's face was so infused with love that Connor could feel an uncomfortable emotion closing his throat.

"And like all beautiful women," Logan said, "she is complicated."

"Now *you* sound like the voice of experience."

For a moment something pained appeared in Logan's eyes, but then he rolled his shoulders and ran a hand through his hair. "You don't find something like this and just keep on as if it's normal. I'll have to notify the authorities. Depending what they decide, the wedding could be delayed."

Connor had let out a long, low whistle, loaded with the sympathy of a man who knew firsthand how the unexpected could mess with a guy's plans.

Then, taking one more look at the fresco,

he had said goodbye to Logan and left the chapel.

Now, days later, lying side by side at the pool with Isabella, with the sun warming their backs, he was feeling that again.

Paralyzed by almost incomprehensible beauty. When Isabella saw how intently he was looking at her, she smiled and didn't look away. Neither did he.

The danger he was in came to him slowly. He'd tried to fight this attraction every way that he knew how. He'd tried to create distance. He'd tried to nip it in the bud. He'd even moved out of her house.

But still, he was falling in love with Isabella Rossi. Or maybe he already had. That was why he had felt such an urgent need to cancel that date, to get out from under the same roof as her. It was why he was in this state of heightened awareness and had been for days. The fact that he could see beauty so intensely was connected to what he was experiencing with this woman.

She reached out and touched his shoulder, and again, because of his heightened awareness, he felt that touch as though he had never been touched before, had never felt so exquisitely connected to another human being before.

"I've gone from being terrified of the water to loving it," she said huskily.

"I know, you have been a great student." He was the wrong man for a woman to love. He had always known that. His childhood had left him wary of relationships, and his choice of work had suited that perfectly. He had told himself he was protecting women from the potential for loss, but in fact he had been protecting himself.

Because he'd always known only the bravest of women could handle what he was dishing out.

True, he wasn't in active service anymore. But what had just gone down in Azerbaijan was plenty of evidence he still had his knack for finding danger.

It seemed to him this little slip of a woman lying on the deck beside him was the bravest of women.

"Connor?"

"Huh?"

"I've never had that before, what I had just now."

"What?"

"Just fun," she said. "Just good old-fashioned

fun. Even when I was a child, Giorgio was my best friend. He couldn't run and play like everyone else, and so I stayed with him. We read and drew pictures, but I've never really had this. Just to let go of everything, to play until I'm so out of breath I feel as if I can't breathe.

"I mean, I do it with my students. I have fun with them, but it's not the same. I have to be the adult. I have to maintain a modicum of control. I don't ever get to be this carefree."

His awareness of her deepened yet again. Her beautiful eyes were sparkling with tears.

"So, thank you," she said. "I'm never going to be able to thank you enough. Never."

His awareness of himself deepened, too, but not in a good way. An unexpected element inserted itself into the pure and sizzling awareness of the moment. Connor suddenly felt ashamed of himself. He'd backed out of that date out of pure terror of what she was doing to him. He'd left her house because he couldn't trust himself around her without wanting to taste her lips again.

But when he'd challenged her to embrace what terrified her, she had done it in a heartbeat. She had shown incredible bravery.

And now she was telling him she'd never had fun. That fooling around in the swimming pool was the most fun she'd ever had. She'd given her whole life to looking after others. Her husband, and then the kids at school.

It seemed to Connor he was being given an opportunity to do something good. Maybe the best thing he'd ever done. It wasn't about whether or not he was comfortable. It wasn't about that at all. That feeling that maybe he was falling for her deepened in him. Didn't that call him to be a better man? Didn't it ask him to be more than he had ever been before. Braver? Stronger? More compassionate?

"You know that date I canceled?" His voice was so low it came out sounding like a whisper.

She went very still.

"You want to give me another chance?"

"Yes," she said, her voice low, too, as if they were in a church. "Yes, I do."

"What about tomorrow night?"

"That would be perfect."

Isabella looked at her bed. It was covered with every single item of clothing that she owned. She had tried on the red dress and then taken it off. He'd already seen it. It wasn't the message she wanted to give. Nothing was the message she wanted to give.

Suddenly, frustrated, exhausted from trying things on and ripping them back off, she threw herself down on the bed, falling backward into the heap of clothes. Isabella lay there, staring at the ceiling.

She thought back over their week of swimming lessons. There had been the most delicious sense of getting to know Connor, of connecting with him. There had been the most delicious awareness of him physically, a yearning to touch him and taste him that was astonishingly powerful. That small kiss had shown her what was going on between them was like riding a wild horse. It wasn't going to be controlled.

She had never felt that for Giorgio.

A stab of guilt pierced her heart. And she had a terrible moment of self-awareness. Giorgio, despite the fact he was dying, had been the safest choice she could make. He had been her friend, and she had loved him as a friend.

But that other kind of love? The kind that was filled with passion and excitement? Hadn't she known from the time she was a little girl that that kind was unpredictable and hurtful and destructive?

Connor would never be unfaithful. After

you knew him for ten minutes, you knew that of him. That he was a man of complete honor.

But he had pitted his formidable strength against the wrongs of the world. He had warned her that he sought out danger, and that he found it. She had seen that for herself when she had caught the tail end of that news clip out of Azerbaijan.

To allow herself to love Connor Benson would be to open herself up to pain such as she had never felt, not even when she was a little girl and had seen her father in a café with a woman who was not her mother.

From the second she had spotted him, Isabella had begun working on an elaborate story: it was someone from work. It was a friend. It was a cousin. And then her father had leaned forward and kissed that woman on the mouth with unmistakable passion.

Then there had been the different pain: watching Giorgio die, every day a series of losses for him, and for them, until she was feeding the man she married baby food from a spoon.

And so, this week Isabella had tackled one of her fears. She had learned to swim. And she had deliberately fanned the fire she had seen in Connor's eyes.

But without considering the consequences. In a way, she had won. He had given in. He had asked her out again after canceling the first time. But was she really ready to open herself to more pain?

Isabella realized, sadly, she had used up all her bravery. She did not have any left. She certainly did not have the kind left that you would need to go on the wild ride that was love.

Not with a man like Connor Benson.

The next morning, she caught up with him on the edge of town. She had known he would be there, heading out for his early morning swim.

"Connor."

He swung around and looked at her. His smile held as much promise as the sun that was just beginning to touch the rooftops of Monte Calanetti.

"I'm sorry. About tonight?"

His smile faded.

"I can't. I realized I have a previous obligation."

He cocked his head at her.

She should have thought of the previous obligation before now! She blurted out the first thing that came to her head. "My students are putting on a skit for the spring fete. I'm not ready. The costumes aren't finished. I haven't started the props."

He was looking at her quietly.

"So, clearly a date is out of the question. For right now."

And in a while, he would be gone, anyway. If she could just hold off for a few more days, she would be what she most liked to be. Safe. She would leave that woman she had been introduced to in Nico's swimming pool behind, a memory that would fade more with each passing day, and then week, and then year.

Besides, neither of them had addressed where a date would be leading—down that dark road to heartbreak? There were so many different routes to get to that destination.

So, if she should be so pleased with herself that she was taking control of a situation that had the potential to get seriously out of control if she let it, why did she feel so annoyed that instead of looking dismayed that she had canceled their date, he looked downright relieved.

"Is it the swimming lessons that put you behind the eight ball?" he asked.

She frowned at him. "What is this? Behind the eight ball?"

"Have you ever played pool?"

"Isn't that what we just did all week?"

He threw back his head and laughed. Oh, of all the things he could have done, that was the worst. It filled her with an ache to live in a state of playful days of hearing him laugh. But of course, given what he did for a living, that was unrealistic.

There would be far more days of waiting for him, of anxiety sitting in her stomach like a pool of acid, of uncertainty and fear.

"In America, we play a variation of billiards called pool. Guys like me who spend ninety-nine percent of our lives bored out of our skulls become very good at it. There's a game in pool called eight ball," he said. "The eight ball is black. You can only touch it when it's the last ball on the table, otherwise you lose. So, if it gets between you and the ball you are aiming at, you are in a very difficult predicament. That's what 'behind the eight ball' means."

"What about the one percent?" she asked. She didn't care about the eight ball.

"Huh?"

"You spend ninety-nine percent of your life bored out of your skull—what about the one percent?"

"Oh, that."

She waited.

He grinned at her, devil-may-care. "It's one percent of all hell breaking loose." He held that smile, but she saw something else in his eyes, as if he held within him shadows of every terrible thing he had ever seen.

"And that's the part you love, and also the part you pay a price for."

He did not like it when the powers of observation that he had encouraged her to hone were turned on him.

"Weren't we talking about you?"

"Yes, we were," she said. "I think that would be an accurate description of how I feel right now, behind this eight ball. I have much to do, and not enough time to do it."

"My fault. Because of the swimming. I'll help you get ready for your skit. I'm winding down on the recon for the wedding anyway. I'll be wrapped up in a couple of days."

And then he would be gone.

CHAPTER EIGHT

"YOU WON'T LIKE IT," Isabella said with all the firmness she could muster. "You won't like helping me. I'm making paper sunshine cut-outs."

Connor laughed again, but she could hear a faint edge to it. "Lady, my life has been so full of things I didn't like it would make your head spin."

Again, that hint of the dark places he had been that he carried within him. "What is this, make your head spin?"

"I'll explain it to you over paper sunshines."

Isabella was ashamed of her weakness. She could not give up what he was offering. She could not give up an opportunity to spend time with him. It seemed to her that she had caught a glimpse of his world when they went swimming. Now she had an overwhelming desire to see how he would react to hers.

No doubt with utter boredom. But at least it was not a date, that event that was so loaded with romantic expectation and foolish hopes.

"All right," she said stiffly. "Come after school. Class gets out at one."

"Okay," he said. He sauntered away, into the magic of Monte Calanetti's dawn, whistling. Whistling! It confirmed that he was not the least distressed that she had canceled the date. The exact opposite, in fact.

He was very punctual, and Connor Benson showed up just as her students were swarming out the door of her classroom. He looked like a ship plowing through the sea of bright blue uniforms. Luigi Caravetti, who always had too much energy, was walking backward, catcalling at one of the girls.

Connor sidestepped him easily, but at that very moment, Luigi swung around and smashed into him.

Connor barely moved, but Luigi fell down. With absolute ease, Connor went down on his haunches, helped the little boy up, picked up the homework Luigi wouldn't do anyway and handed it back to him. Luigi said something to him and then wound up and kicked Connor in the shin and ran off before Isabella could reprimand him.

Rubbing his shin, he turned to her and grinned ruefully.

"I'm sorry," she said, "Luigi is a bit of a handful. What did he say to you?"

"I don't know. He said it in Italian. I'm beginning to pick up a few phrases, so I think he told me to watch were I was going. And then he switched to English."

"He doesn't know any English."

"Ah, well, there's a universal word that all little boys—and most big ones—love to use."

"Oh! I will speak to him tomorrow."

"No, that's okay. He kind of reminded me of me at that age. And if I was going to guess something about him? No dad in the picture."

Again, Isabella was taken by Connor's incredible powers of observation. "That's true. In fact, his poor mother had to get a court order to keep the father away from them. He's not, apparently, a very nice man. But still, Luigi is troubled about it all. Children are always troubled about difficulties between their parents."

The last of the children clattered down the stairway to the main floor of the school, and they were cloaked in sudden silence. Then Connor Benson was in her classroom.

"So," he said, putting his hands in his pockets and rocking back on his heels, "this is your world."

"Ninety-nine percent boring," she told him. "One percent all hell breaking loose."

Connor gave her an odd look that she interpreted as *you don't have a clue what all hell breaking loose looks like.* But then he shrugged it off, as if he had given himself a mental order to lighten up. "I'm going to guess that one percent is largely your little Luigi."

"You would be guessing right."

"Nobody asked me what I was doing here when I came in," he said.

"Sorry?"

"When I came in and asked for your classroom, no one at the office asked me what I wanted or what I was doing at the school. They didn't even ask to see identification."

"Obviously we are in need of a security expert!" she said brightly, but he didn't seem amused. She became more serious. "We haven't experienced the kinds of problems here that you have in America."

Did he mutter *yet* under his breath? He removed his hands from his pockets and turned away from her and wandered around her classroom. At first she thought he was looking at drawings and pictures, and she was pleased that he was curious about her world. But then Isabella realized that Connor actually seemed to be looking for something else. She was not sure what.

He stood at the front, taking note of both the doors into the room. Then she saw him go to the windows, open the lock on one. He slid the window open and leaned out, looking at the ground.

He came to the table at the back, where she had the project laid out. He seemed faintly uneasy, but he lifted a sun with the hole in the center and put his head through it, attached the elastic around his chin.

She had planned to be so reserved, professional, accepting his help as a volunteer, but nothing more. Instead, she giggled at the picture this big self-assured man made with his face poking through a hole in a cardboard sunshine. The wall came tumbling down as she joined him at the art table at the back of the room.

How could he wear that silly thing with such aplomb? That's what confidence did, she supposed. "Boys are sunshine," she said.

"And girls?"

She picked up a pink flower and put her

head through the center of it and attached the elastic. "Girls are flowers."

He smiled at her, but she still thought she detected faint uneasiness in him. Well, was that so unusual? Many men seemed uneasy in classrooms. The furniture was all in miniature, after all. The spaces were too tiny for most men, and Connor was even larger than most men.

"These are done," Isabella said, resting her hand on one stack, "but we have seven sunshines remaining to cut out and thirteen flowers. The children drew their own, but the cutting part can be quite difficult for little hands. The cardboard is a bit thick." She gave him a pair of scissors.

He sank into one of the little chairs. She actually wondered if it would break under his weight.

"That doesn't look very comfortable."

"I'm used to discomfort." Connor picked up a particularly messy-looking sun drawn on yellow construction paper.

"Luigi's?" he guessed.

She lifted a shoulder—*yes*.

When they had been swimming, that task had occupied them and filled the space between them. There had been no need for conversation on a personal level.

Now, tongue caught slightly between his teeth as he tried to fit his hands in the little scissors, Connor said, "So, tell me everything."

"What?"

"Where you grew up, how many kids are in your family, what your favorite color is and what your most secret dream is."

Again, she had the feeling he might be trying to distract her from some uneasiness he was feeling. Still, she was happy to do that and so, with his encouragement, she talked. It was amazingly comfortable sitting at the little table, cutting with little scissors, the sun pouring in around them. She marveled at how good it felt to be with him like this, at ease, and yet not at ease the way she had been with Giorgio.

With Connor, something sizzled in the air between them. All that time in the pool together had increased her awareness of him, and that did not change now that they were sitting in her classroom, in chairs too small for them, fully clothed.

She answered all his questions except one. He didn't miss that, of course.

"And is there a secret dream?"

She thought of the way she had felt when she had learned Marianna was pregnant. Happy for Marianna, of course, and yet...

"No," she croaked.

His scissors stopped moving. He looked across at her. "There is," he said.

"I've given up on the secret dream thing."

"Ah." He obviously did not believe her, but he didn't press. They finished all the costume pieces, and he helped her build a simple set.

How could it be both so easy and so difficult to be with him? He came into her world of paper and glue and paint as easily as she had gone into his world of water. And he did the same thing to it.

An existence that had seemed mundane suddenly sparkled. There was laughter everywhere.

Except as he got ready to leave. He was suddenly very serious. "Can you request a different classroom?" he asked.

"What? Why?"

He shrugged and shoved his hands in his pockets. "You should just ask for one on the first floor, if you can."

"I like this one," she said, feeling stubborn.

"I'm sure you do. Unless there's a fire." His

voice, which had been laughter filled only moments ago, was suddenly very grim.

Now, a few days after they had begun, they stood back from her completed set, costumes and props. The set was lightweight cardboard so that it could be moved easily to the village square the day of the fete.

She sighed with contentment. With his help, it was so much better than anything she could have ever done alone.

He stood beside her. "It's done to your satisfaction?"

"Yes. A whole two days before the fete. I am officially out from under the eight ball."

"That's good," he said. "Because now we can have our date."

She slid him a look. He was covered with splotches of blue paint from painting the sky. He had a relaxed smile on his face.

She was so aware of him. It was dangerous. But she had no fight left in her. She did not want to fight anymore. She wanted to see what would happen between them.

Even if it was the most dangerous thing of all.

"Did you have something in mind?" she asked. Her voice sounded like a mouse squeaking.

"Oh, yeah," he said.

"What?" She hoped he would say something safe, something not that different than watching television at her house. A movie, maybe.

"I want to surprise you with it."

"How do I know what to wear for a surprise?" she asked.

"Anything you wear will be fine."

Did he not understand women at all? "If you could give me a hint," she suggested.

"It will have something to do with the chapel."

"The chapel?" Isabella could not imagine what he had in mind. The last time she had seen it, the chapel had looked like a construction site, surrounded by scaffolding.

"Trust me."

"All right."

"I'll pick you up just before eight."

"All right."

It was complete surrender, and she knew it. And looking at his face, so familiar to her now, she realized it was a surrender for him, too. It was a surrender to what had been building between them like a thunderstorm on the horizon.

Looking at his face, Isabella wondered

when exactly this had happened. When had he come to feel beloved to her?

Had it been as he painted the sky on cardboard or cut the head hole from yet another sunshine? Or had it been before that, when he had drawn her into the swimming pool and taught her to embrace what frightened her most?

Maybe it was before even that. Maybe it had begun that morning they had walked through the dawn to the river and she had felt the mud ooze up between her toes.

Or maybe it had been from the very first moment, when she had put his breakfast outside his door and been assaulted by him in her own home, the beginning of the waking up that had led to this: how she loved her life with Connor Benson in it.

It was a warm evening, so Isabella wore a simple white sundress of eyelet cotton, with narrow straps and a ribbon at the waist and a wide skirt. It did not sing the siren song that her red dress had, but it showed off her coloring and her figure, and it was more her, somehow. It was as if, with Connor, she was exploring herself and slowly arriving at what that really was.

She saw she had chosen exactly the right

ensemble when he arrived at her door. She could see it in his eyes even before he told her that she looked beautiful. Connor looked extraordinary. She had always seen him looking quite casual. Tonight he was in pressed dark slacks and a cream-colored linen dress shirt.

He went down her narrow walk before her and held open a car door. It was a very sleek, sporty car.

"Did you have a car before?" He hadn't ever parked one when he lived with her.

"I had one at my disposal, if I needed it. I prefer to walk. It gives me a better sense of a place. You notice more."

"Is this the car you had?" she asked.

He shook his head. "I traded up."

"Why?" she whispered, looking at the sleek gray convertible with awe.

"It seems to me, my lady, you have missed a few things on the road to romance. Your man wants to show you new worlds and impress you."

Her man? On the road to romance? Was she really ready for this? Isabella could barely breathe as he held open the door for her. It seemed like a long step down into the low-slung sports car, and he took her hand and helped her. She settled back in a deep leather seat.

The car was a dream to ride in, and she loved the way Connor handled it in the narrow streets. There was nothing about him, she realized, that was inclined to show off. And yet he was obviously extremely confident and capable handling the very powerful car. She loved the way one hand rested lightly on the wheel, his other on the knob of the gearshift. The ride seemed over way too soon. When she reached for the door handle, he gave her a meaningful look and she let her hand fall away.

He opened the door for her and then went around to the trunk and opened it as well. He looped the handle of a large wicker basket over his left arm and offered her his right. She threaded her arm through the crook of his elbow and they went up the well-worn path to the palazzo's chapel.

It was as she had remembered, almost completely engulfed in scaffolding.

"It must be American," she said out loud.

"What?"

"A date at a construction site."

"What? Italians don't date at construction sites?" He shook his head, teasing her. "I thought you people had perfected the romantic gesture."

"Why would you think that?"

"My mother calls Italy the land of *amore*."

The land of *amore*. She lived here, and she had missed it! Not that she was going to admit that to Connor.

And then he led her around the back of the chapel.

Isabella gasped. There was a table set up there with a white tablecloth on it. It faced out over a view that seemed to show the rolling, vineyard-covered hills of the entire valley.

Connor placed his picnic basket on the table and pulled back a chair for her. "The sun will be setting—" he glanced at his watch "—in seven minutes. Do you want a glass of wine?"

How could she refuse? He took a bottle out of his basket, dewdrops of condensation running down it. He popped the cork with complete ease. While the wine breathed, he took long-stemmed glasses, plates and cutlery from the bag.

He glanced at his watch. She could see the sun beginning to lower to the edges of the hills. The light was changing, softening all around them.

"What I want to share with you is this

way," he said. "I'll let the wine breathe for a moment before I pour it."

What did he mean? The sun would go down over there, in front of them. Was that not what he had brought her here to see, a most wildly romantic gesture? She turned and looked at him. He held out his hand to her, and she took it. Could she ever get used to the feeling of a hand like his closing around hers?

He led her around the chapel and in a side door.

The light inside was suddenly drenched in color, golds and pinks. It was almost as though the chapel had been designed for this moment in time: the setting of the sun. Despite much evidence of work and restoration, when it was suffused with light like this the space seemed sacred.

"I wanted you to see this," he said, and with a sweep of his arm directed her gaze to the side wall of the chapel, by the family pews.

She saw a fresco on the wall of the chapel. Even without the amazing addition of the light from the setting sun, the fresco took her breath away. She moved toward it as if in a dream, staring at the scene before her with utter awe.

The detail of the Madonna and child was

stunning: as if each hair on their heads, each eyelash, had been painted individually.

"The color is astounding," she breathed. Connor was standing right beside her, gazing at the fresco. "Their skin, the color of her robe, the child's lips."

Both Madonna and child had enormous, expressive eyes turned to the heavens, where the clouds parted and a beam of light illuminated them.

"Do you think I can touch it?" she whispered.

"I think so."

She placed her hand on the wall. The sun was touching the wall, and its warmth had seeped into it, making the fresco seem even more like a living thing. "I don't think I've ever seen anything as beautiful as this."

His hand covered hers. "I know. I felt the same way when I saw it. It's been covered all these years. I can't imagine why, and yet it probably preserved the magnificence of the colors. You know, Isabella, I have seen the world at its ugly worst, and I'm not sure why but this restored something in me."

"I understand."

"Do you?"

"Yes, it's like it holds a message. That

beauty survives, or wins. It's like it is saying, when all else falls away, the best, the good, will remain."

"That's exactly what I felt when I saw it, not that I could articulate it like that."

"The best," she said quietly, "a mother's love for her child. The Madonna radiates love. Maybe not just for the child. Something bigger. For the world." She could feel the tears clogging her throat, and she bit them back. Even so, he seemed to know what an emotional moment this was for her, because his hand came to rest on the small of her back.

Time slipped away as they explored the fresco together, pointing out incredible details they thought the other might have missed.

Finally, when darkness had fallen so completely that the church was pitched in blackness, Connor ushered her back outside.

He poured the wine and took some candles out of the basket, placed them carefully on the table and lit them. And then he took a dish of still-hot pasta out, wrapped in a tea towel. When he took the towel off, the spicy fragrance of the lasagna made her mouth water. She was not sure if it was because of the painting or because of him that the food

tasted as if the angels themselves had prepared it.

"Tell me now about your secret dream,"
he said softly.

The night was so perfect. Seeing the fresco
had brought her secret dreams to the forefront
of her mind. It felt right to give him all of her,
to hold nothing back.

"Once, I dreamed I would have babies,"
she confessed.

"Not now? I can picture you with babies.
I can picture that look on your face, exactly
like the one on the face of the Madonna in
the chapel."

"I'm getting very old for this dream," she
said, her voice small.

"You think thirty-three is old for having
babies?"

"Isn't it?"

He actually laughed. "My mother had my
half brother Sammy when she was thirty-six,
and my sister, Amelia, a year later. The baby
of the family, Henry, arrived when she was
forty."

"Thank you for telling me that. It just
feels as if everyone having babies is so much
younger than me. Marianna's shower is tomorrow night, and I was trying to think of

reasons not to go. Of course, I could not think of a reason not to go that would not raise eyebrows. In Monte Calanetti, celebrating the coming of a baby is mandatory, like giving kisses to strangers on New Year's Eve. But it is very painful watching others have what I wanted."

"You are not kissing any strangers on New Year's Eve," he teased.

Isabella shivered. Would it be reading too much into the teasingly possessive statement to think she could count on Connor to still be part of her life as the village welcomed the new year?

His teasing tone was gone when he spoke again. "Isabella, you and your husband could not have children?"

She shook her head. "He was already too sick by the time we married."

"Aw, Isabella."

"Please don't say that as if I'm to be pitied."

"I'm sorry, that wasn't my intention."

"I wanted to try, even though I knew I would be raising a child alone. Is that selfish?"

"It makes me wonder why you wanted one so badly that you would be willing to raise it alone. That is the hardest thing. I know, because I watched my mom do it. Even if there had been financial security, which I am sure you would have, the emotional burden is huge. The responsibility is a lot to carry alone."

"I see that every day in Luigi," she said.

"And yet?" Connor heard the unspoken as clearly as if she had said it.

She drew in a deep breath. The stars and the wine and the gaze of Connor, steady and strong, drew her every secret out of her soul.

"And yet, I have always craved a family. A real family."

"Yours wasn't?"

"Oh, my mother and my father stayed together, but only because they both considered it a sin to split up. Our family was a sham. My father always had girlfriends, mistresses. My mother lived in a state of wounded pride and furious anger."

"I'm sorry."

"It's no matter," she said. "Not now. I have my students. They are all my children now. I am lucky in so many ways. And you, Connor? What are your thoughts on children?"

"My own?" he asked. His voice broke in pretended terror, and she laughed, but she was unwilling to let him off the hook so easily.

"I think you would make a wonderful father," she said.

"How, when I have never had that modeled for me?"

"Yes, you have, by men you admired, if not by your own father. I can tell by how you taught me to swim how good you would be at it."

"That's what my mom says, too, when she sees me tussling with my new brothers and sister, that I'd make a great daddy."

"You enjoy being with them?"

"Don't tell anyone, but it's one of my favorite things."

"And why would you not want to tell anyone this?"

"Kind of spoils the whole warrior image. But seriously? I don't think my lifestyle is very conducive to children."

"I think you're wrong. Your lifestyle is about honor, and about standing strong for what you believe. I am not sure you could give a child any greater gift than that."

"Until you come home in a box."

"What is this? Come home in a box?"

"It means to not come home at all."

Isabella wanted to shudder at the harshness of the expression, but she reminded herself there was no room in this man's life for a woman who shuddered at harsh realities.

"And just like that," he continued quietly, "you've made a lot of pain in the world. You've made a Luigi."

"Or maybe, if the love was strong enough, you've left a legacy that is not like the legacy poor Luigi has inherited."

"Maybe," he said, but he did not sound convinced.

The wind came up suddenly and lifted the tablecloth and blew out the candle. By the time they had rearranged the cloth and relit the candle, the serious mood was gone. They joked back and forth while they ate, and when silence fell it was comfortable, soaking up the beauty of the night skyline and the immense sky overhead and the stars that studded it.

Then he slipped his phone from his pocket. She was almost relieved he had made such a wildly inappropriate gaffe in the evening, because she thought to believe in perfection was probably an invitation to fate to prove you wrong. But then Connor searched through the phone and found some music. He put it on, then pushed another button. The phone glowed softly.

"How did you do that?" she asked.

"It's an app—it turns your phone into a light."

"Americans," she teased.

"Yes, we have to have all the state-of-the-art toys."

"If it brings you happiness."

"Isabella, stuff does not bring happiness. This brings happiness." He rose from the table, and he set his phone on the table and held out his hand to her.

"Dance with me?"

She rose from the table and went into his arms with a sigh.

"No words," he said of the music choice. "Not English, and not Italian. I think music and art can speak the language of the heart."

With the stars watching them and tears spilling down her cheeks at the absolute and complete wonder of this moment, Isabella Rossi luxuriated in the feeling of Connor Benson's arms closing around her. Her cheek was pressed into his chest, and she could feel the steady beat of his heart in her skin.

It was homecoming.

It was as if every event of her entire life had served only one purpose and that was to lead her to this moment, dancing under the stars of a Tuscan sky with Connor swaying against her, his hand on the small of her back, his breath fanning the hair on the top of her head.

One song became another. She kicked off her shoes. So did he. The grass was sweet and cool under their feet.

And then, in one smooth movement, he released one of her hands and bent down and retrieved his phone. He shut off the music and the light, plunging them into darkness and silence.

Only it wasn't really silent. She could hear the sounds of the night insects chirping and rubbing their wings, the call of a night bird. She could hear her own breath. And his. She was certain she could hear the beating of her own heart.

It was no more completely dark than it was completely silent. The houses in the vineyards on the hillsides were matched by the pinpricks of light that shined brilliantly in the black velvet sky above them. His face was illuminated in a sliver of moonlight. She reached up and touched his features, running her fingertips along his forehead and his temples, the bridge of his nose, the faint scrape of whiskers on his cheek.

And then her fingers found the silky plumpness of his lower lip, and he reached out and held her hand there, kissed her fingertips and moaned with a sound of such yearning and longing it sent a wave of tingles up her spine.

His eyes on hers, he turned her hand over and kissed the palm, and the inside of her wrist, and up the length of her arm, feathery little kisses that the stars that watched over them would have approved of. He put that hand away from him and took up her other one and kissed it, just as thoroughly.

And then he tugged, urging her against the length of him.

She went willingly. She'd had hints of what this would feel like—accidental brushings at the pool, going by him in a narrow hallway— but she could not stop herself from sighing at how they fit together so perfectly, how the hard wall of him felt with her body pressed against it. She wrapped her arms around him, melding herself into his contours.

His hands moved her hair away from her face, and then his right index finger went to her chin and tilted it up.

He scanned her face, drank it in. She saw

the same look of reverence that she had seen when he looked at the fresco.

"Would it be all right if I kissed you?" he asked huskily.

CHAPTER NINE

OF COURSE IT would not be all right if Connor Benson kissed her, Isabella thought dreamily. Her world would never be the same. It would open places in her that could not be forced shut again. But already her body was trembling in anticipation of welcoming him, and so instead of answering with words, she rose up on the tiptoes of her bare feet and took his lips.

They tasted of wine and starlight and pure masculine perfection. Connor's lips tasted of everything that was beautiful about the world. Everything.

He tangled his hands ever so gently in her hair and tilted his head over hers. The plundering was sweet, his lips claiming her lips, his tongue probing the curves and hollows of her lips and then of her mouth. She could feel the gentle scrape of his whiskers against the tender skin of her face.

She was rocketed into a different world. She was not so much Isabella, and he was not so much Connor. It was more as if they were part of some enormous energy that fused. That energy had been fusing since the dawn of time, drawing men and women together in a way that guaranteed the future of the human race.

That's how big what was between them was: the whole human race relied on this fusion that was searing, delightful and painful by turns.

It opened up a cavernous hunger in her, to know more, to be more, to be filled to the top. It left her with an aching awareness that until this moment, she had been empty.

She released him and staggered back a step, touching her lips, her eyes wide and searching on his face.

"What?" he whispered.

"I didn't know." And then she was crying again, the night pregnant with overwhelming emotion. "I didn't know that it could be this beautiful."

He reached out over the distance she had created between them, pulled her back gently against his chest, stroked her hair as her tears soaked his shirt. "Shh," he said. "Shh, it's going to be okay."

A star a million years away fell through the night sky, leaving a stunning trail of light behind it.

And she thought that was what she had never really believed. Not in her whole life. She had never really believed it could be okay.

She went to take his lips again, but he shook his head, tucked her head to his chest and continued to stroke her hair.

"I don't think we should start again," he said huskily. He released her, turned to the table and began to pack their things back in the basket.

She hugged herself. A whisper of a breeze touched her, and she felt chilly without the protection of his embrace.

"Why?" Her voice, in her own ears, sounded like a mew of pure need.

"I don't want you to look back and regret an impulse."

"I won't."

"If it's not an impulse, you will still feel the same way tomorrow night," he said.

"I resent that you are choosing now to show off how disciplined you are." She went up behind him and pressed herself into his back, reached around and ran her hand over the marvelous strength of his forearms.

He went very still, and then he turned from

the table and caught her up. He kissed her again, but lightly this time, before putting her away from him.

"Tomorrow," he promised her huskily. "Tomorrow night. We could have a second date."

"There is no tomorrow night," she said, aware her tone was sulky. "I have to go to Marianna's shower. As much as I would like to get out of it, I cannot."

"Well, then Sunday. Your day off, correct? We could spend the day together."

"It's the fete."

"Ah."

"Will you come watch?"

"I wouldn't miss it for anything. And after the fete? Are you free?"

"Yes." She felt shy and pleased. She actually felt grateful to him that he had stopped the runaway train of their passion, slowed it down. She thought it showed enormous respect for her.

"Would you let me plan something for after? That will be our second date."

"Yes," she said, and her sigh of happiness felt like that star she had watched fall from the sky.

When Connor woke the next morning, it seemed to him his whole body was smiling.

And that was even though he did not really like his accommodations.

There had not been much available when he had taken his hurried leave from Isabella's house, a small, dark room at the back of someone's house. But it had its own bathroom and a separate entrance and compared to some of the places he had laid his head in his life, it was a palace.

And last night he had been more than grateful that he was not staying under Isabella's roof. Where would that have gone?

Where was it going, anyway? Apparently, at his instigation, it was going to a second official date.

How was he going to live up to the first date? Because really, in the date department, he was pretty sure he had scored a perfect ten, following Justin's instructions to be original.

He wondered what he should do next. But then that question pestered him again. Where was it going, anyway?

He realized, stunned, that he knew where it was going. He knew exactly. It was why he had refused to follow that kiss everywhere it had wanted to go.

He wanted to marry her.

Connor knew he would never feel right

about having her in the way he wanted her without doing everything right. She was that kind of woman. Without saying a word she demanded a certain standard. Yes, she had a passionate side, and yes, that was easy to coax to the surface.

She would never be a quick roll in the hay. Underneath that passion, she was old-fashioned and traditional. She was the kind of woman who demanded a man's respect without ever saying a word out loud. With Isabella Rossi, you would either be committed for life or you shouldn't even be playing ball.

Committed for life. He mulled that over. The very thought a month ago would have put him on a plane for anywhere.

But now he was thinking how easy it would be for him to adapt to life in Monte Calanetti. With phones and computers being so high-tech, with global travel being so easy, there was no reason he could not work with Justin and Itus from here.

He even thought that children, whom, with the exception of his half siblings, he'd always found mildly repulsive, would be something he could manage with Isabella guiding him through the pitfalls. Maybe they could have a little girl who looked like her. What if the little girl looked like him, though? Maybe they would be better off to have a little boy.

He got up out of bed, filled with restless energy. He knew how to deal with restless energy, or thought he did. Connor gathered his swim things.

But somehow he never made it to the river. He was stopped by wildflowers that grew by the road. He wasn't going to see her tonight. She was going to a shower. He wouldn't repeat his performance from last time she had gone to a function—he wouldn't be chasing through the streets looking for her.

He would leave the flowers for her to find after school. He wanted her to know he was thinking about her. Bonus: they would make her think of him, too.

Though, when he thought of the reluctance with which she had broken away from their first real kiss, he was happily aware she might not be thinking of much else except him! Being romantic—the thing he'd run in terror from his whole life—had the potential to be all kinds of fun.

He began to plan their second date in earnest. Connor wanted to do even better than he had done on the first one. She would want to relax after all her hard work on the fete.

And so he spent the next few hours figuring out where to get a canoe. They would explore the river and find the perfect place, a secluded meadow of wildflowers that could only be reached by the boat.

They would have a picnic supper there. He planned an exquisite menu. He thought of introducing her to the mystical experience of swimming in the dark. And then he would paddle them home, the water so inky dark it would reflect the stars. He hoped he could create the illusion they were paddling through the heavenly night sky.

He left a second vase of flowers on her doorstep, where she would find it immediately after the shower. It contained a note telling her to bring her swimsuit for their second date after the fete. He underlined *swim* so that she wouldn't get any ideas about tormenting him with one of those bikinis.

But then, on thinking about it, he did not want to be in a secluded meadow with her in a bikini. So he tore up that note, and made a new one that simply said what time he would pick her up. He hesitated a long time. Should he conclude with *I love you*? He tried it. And then felt foolish. He tore up that note, too.

On the other hand, he wanted her to know

he was serious. He wanted her to know the whole course of his life felt as if it was changing. He tried a third time.

Dear Isabella,
Life is a river, with calm places and turbulent places. I wonder if you would like to join me on this wild and unpredictable ride? If you are willing, I will pick you up tomorrow evening, after the fete, and we will explore the river.

Instead of signing it with "love," he drew a clumsy heart and signed his name.

He stuffed the note in the vase of flowers before he could change his mind.

And then he went shopping for a swimsuit for Isabella, uncaring of the raised eyebrows and giggles as he went through the selection of women's bathing suits, noting the selection in Monte Calanetti at this time of year was quite a bit better than Isabella had claimed it was.

He purchased a particularly dowdy suit, put the wrapped package under his arm and went back to his humble quarters. He could not wait for tomorrow to come.

As Connor arrived at the town square the

next night, it was already filling up with people. A makeshift stage had been set up at the far end of the square, and someone was testing a sound system.

For the first time since he had started planning the second date, he came down to earth. Connor could feel some nervousness tickle along his spine at the number of people in the square. As far as he could see, there was absolutely no security for the event. Didn't the good people of Monte Calanetti know that there were no safe places anymore? Not in the whole world?

He scanned the crowd and relaxed marginally. Really, it was just a family event. The chairs set up in neat rows in front of the stage were nearly full already, but no one seemed to mind. Farther back from the stage area, families were setting up picnic blankets. There were grandmothers and grandfathers, women holding babies, and children threading through the crowd screaming their delight. Young men stood in defensive huddles trying to pretend they did not notice the young women who sashayed by them in their spring clothes.

For all that it seemed benign and happy, Connor could not make himself go into the square and that crush of people to look for one of the remaining seats. He found a tree just on the very edge of the square, leaned his shoulder up against it and watched from a distance.

He could see the kids from Isabella's school, already seated cross-legged on the ground up front, in front of the rows of chairs. He spotted her class easily, their sunshine and flower headdresses making them stand out from the others.

There was Isabella, pacing up front, bending over to adjust a headpiece here, to tap a shoulder there, to smile encouragement or to listen to what one of the children was saying.

She looked extraordinary in a simple shift.

He realized there was no hope at all that the bathing suit he had chosen for her was going to dim her light. She could have been wearing a burlap sack today and she would have looked beautiful.

She was absolutely glowing.

Was that because she had feelings for him that matched his growing feelings for her? Did that light that shined forth from her like a beacon of hope have something to do with him? Did it have something to do with that kiss at the chapel? It felt like quite something to be responsible for a light like that one.

She turned suddenly, as if she could feel the intensity of his gaze on her. Her eyes scanned the crowd and then she saw him.

Despite all the noise and motion that separated them, it was as if the world went still. Her eyes locked on his. She lifted a hand in shy acknowledgment. He lifted his back. She smiled, and the glow about her deepened. She turned back to her responsibilities.

And he turned back to his. He tried to relax, but it was not in his nature. He simply could not be in a situation like this and not be scanning, watching for trouble. It had been a part of his life for too long.

A band took the stage and began to play boisterously, if without great talent. They received wild applause and launched into their second number.

Connor noticed something. His eyes rested on a man who, like Connor, was on the fringes of the crowd. The man was by himself in a sea of families.

The band finished their second number to wild applause, took bows and began to pack up their things. Two of Isabella's children, little girls in matching pink dresses, carried the cardboard backdrop for their performance onto the stage. Isabella's class rose in preparation.

Connor watched, and then his gaze went back to the man. He frowned. It was a very warm day. Why was that man wearing an overcoat? Why was he looking around like that, furtively?

The band had vacated the stage and Isabella's class marched into their places. The boys with their sunshine heads were in the back, the girls in the front. They were so excited, joyous in their moment of being at the center.

Isabella stood off to one side. She darted forward and made a last adjustment and said a stern word to a boy whose sun was looking decidedly crumpled. Connor recognized Luigi, the boy who had run into him and then told him to watch where he was going.

And then she went back to the side again and nodded. She beamed with pride as those innocent young voices filled the air.

Connor did not have to speak Italian to know the song welcomed spring. The suns rose, and the flowers waved happily.

But he was not transported to that place of innocence and hope. In fact, he felt as if the music and the rising suns and the waving flowers were all fading. Because the man was moving through the crowd, snaking his way in and out of the crush of people.

Connor pushed himself away from the tree he had been leaning on. With a sense of urgency, he closed the distance between them, following the man through the crowd. Connor ignored the outrage when he blocked people's views.

The man was nearly in front of the stage now, where the children had been sitting moments ago. He was reaching inside his coat pocket.

Without hesitation, Connor became that huge mountain lion he had been nicknamed for. He went from stalking to pouncing. He launched himself at the man in the coat. They went down in the front of the crowd of people. Everyone was screaming in Italian. The commotion moved like a wave through the crowd until it reached the stage. Isabella, who had been focused on the children, turned, as if in slow motion. Her mouth formed a surprised O. The singing faltered and then ground to a halt.

Connor rolled back to his feet, taking the other man with him. He lifted him up by the collar of the too-warm coat and reached his hand into the pocket. His hand closed around something cold and square.

Wrong shape.

Connor tugged it out and glared at his hand. There was a camera in it.

Connor stared at it. And then, convinced there was danger, he ripped open the buttons of the too-warm jacket. A wrapped birthday gift was hidden in the folds and fell to the ground.

"What's this?" he asked. It looked innocuous, but his training told him it could be anything. The whole point was to make dangerous things appear innocuous.

The man was staring at him with incomprehension. Connor picked up the package, and held it in front of him. "What is this?" he demanded again.

He was hit in the knees from behind and staggered forward a step before whirling to face this new opponent.

Luigi, was there, his face as crumpled as his sunshine headdress. He was screaming in Italian. The man was talking rapidly, both hands raised at his sides, open palmed.

Connor recognized *ma sei pazzo*.

And then Isabella was there, her hands

resting gently on Luigi's shoulders. The little boy turned to her skirt and wept.

She said something to the man in Italian, and seeing her embracing the boy, he thrust the wrapped parcel into Connor's arms and turned and pushed his way through the crowd.

Isabella's eyes, distressed, went to Connor's face. "Luigi's dad," she said quietly. "He wanted a picture of his son in the fete. He wanted to give him a birthday present."

Luigi sobbed something against her skirt, and she stroked his head.

"His dad wasn't allowed to go to his birthday party," she said sadly.

And then a woman pushed her way through the milling, jabbering crowd and grabbed Luigi away from Isabella. The woman turned and marched through the crowd, her chin tilted proudly, half holding Luigi's hand, half dragging him.

"How does this happen?" Isabella whispered. "Presumably they loved each other once. How does it turn to this?"

And then she brushed at her skirt and smiled weakly at Connor. He shoved his hands in his pockets and rocked back on his heels, weathering the dirty looks of the crowd returning to their seats.

"I will see if the children will go on," Isabella said. "I think that would be best, don't you?"

He nodded and watched her weave her way back through the crowd, get onstage and shepherd those distressed children. In minutes, she had comforted them enough that they were able to resume their song.

She had not, Connor noted, said one word of recrimination toward him over his overreaction to what had happened.

But then, she didn't have to. He had enough recrimination for both of them. He made his way through the crowds, holding the birthday present along with the parcel containing the bathing suit for Isabella, which he had retrieved. No one even seemed to notice him.

This was Italy. He supposed there were passionate disruptions all the time. But that did not make him feel one bit better.

What he felt was that he had been living in a fool's paradise. Was he really tangling their lives together when she had no idea what she was letting herself in for?

He went to her house, not knowing what to do with the gift for Luigi except drop it off there. He saw his vase of flowers waiting there for her, and in a moment of pure frustration, he swept them off her stoop with his shoe.

The glass shattered and flowers were strewn everywhere. His note was soaked in water. Annoyed with himself, he set Luigi's gift inside her door. Her door was unlocked, of course—this was Monte Calanetti, and the only person in the whole town who was out of step was him. He found her broom and dustpan and swept up the mess he had made and put it in the bin under her sink.

He told himself to leave. He could do what needed to be done over the phone. It would be better that way.

But he did not leave. He went through her house, stood in the doorway of the bedroom he had used and thought of the journey they had been on since that first morning when he had thought she was an assailant.

Normal people did not think like that. Normal people did not go into schools and look for escape routes and try to figure out how you would get out of the building if it burned. Normal people did not drag men in overcoats to the ground in town squares.

From that first day, he should have backed off. What had he done, pressing forward instead?

He stood for a moment in the doorway leading to the bathroom. The showerhead had been fixed, and a new curtain and rod had been installed. The curtain was no longer transparent, and under different circumstances that might have made him smile. But now, standing here, he could remember her wrapped in her shower curtain, and all he felt was an abject sense of loss.

He went back downstairs and stood in her kitchen, memorizing it and saying goodbye.

And then the door squeaked open behind him.

"Hello, Connor."

He turned and looked at her. He had hoped to avoid her. And at the same time, he had hoped for one last chance to look at her.

Just like looking at her house, he realized he was trying to memorize every single thing about her: the upward tilt of her eyes, the puffiness of her bottom lip, the shine of her hair. He was trying to both burn it into his memory and say—

"Goodbye, Isabella."

She looked as if he had struck her. "Goodbye? But—"

"I have to go," he said.

"Go?"

"I'm leaving Monte Calanetti."

"Leaving Monte Calanetti?" she asked, distressed. "But why?"

She had to ask that? After the mistake he had just made at the fete? After he had overreacted so hugely to Luigi's father? After he had destroyed the performance she had worked so hard on? After he had embarrassed himself and her in front of the whole town?

"I've finished the reconnaissance for the wedding." He could hear the chill in his voice. He put up the shield in his eyes. "I'll be back a week before to put everything in place, and then the day it's over, I'll be gone again."

"But isn't this a bit sudden? I thought…" Her voice drifted away. He hated himself for what he had led her to believe.

But wasn't the truth that he hated himself anyway?

"I'm not who you think I am," he said gruffly.

"I have never met anyone less capable of subterfuge than you!" she snapped. "I know exactly who you are, Connor Benson."

For a moment, everything in him went weak. To have this, to have someone know everything about you, and care anyway? Wasn't that what every man really desired?

Beyond anything else, beyond wealth, beyond accomplishment, beyond success, did not the most humble of dreams live in every man? To be cared about for exactly who he was?

But Connor knew, in his case, that was not possible. When Isabella knew the truth, she would not feel the same about him anymore. How could she? He had never felt the same about himself again.

"Isabella, I need to tell you something."

CHAPTER TEN

I NEED TO tell you something. Isabella felt as if her world was going dark and swinging crazily around her. Hadn't every horrible event of her life begun with those words?

Her father, looking up in that café and seeing her standing there, tears rolling down her face, running across the street to her.

I need to tell you something. This is how it is for a man. It doesn't mean I don't love your mother. And you.

Giorgio, just turned sixteen, *I need to tell you something. I have an illness. I have always known I was not well. I might have ten years. And I might not.*

And now this. Isabella pulled one of her chairs out from the table and sank into it. She was so filled with dread she felt as if she could not breathe.

"What? What do you need to tell me?"

He pulled out the chair across from her. Was she ever going to be able to come into this kitchen, this house, again without seeing him here, remembering him? Because he was saying goodbye.

Connor had a dark secret, just as all the men in her life had had dark secrets. She should have known, should never have left herself open to it. Never.

"It's another woman, isn't it?" she asked, her voice shaking. "Of course! How could I have been so naive to think a man like you could love only me?"

He swore under his breath. "It's not another woman."

"You're dying, then," she decided.

"No. I need to tell you why I left the SEALs," he said.

She perked up. Why he'd left his previous job? That didn't sound as if it could be too bad.

"You need to know what kind of man I really am."

"I already know what kind of man you are," she said.

"No, you don't," he said harshly.

The harshness in Connor's voice made her want to cover up her ears so she didn't have to listen to him. It didn't really matter how bad she thought it was. It mattered how bad he thought it was.

"My team had a tough assignment on the Pakistan-Afghan border." He wouldn't look at her. He was looking at his hands. His fingers kept threading and then unthreading. "It was a hotbed of all kinds of activity. We'd gotten some intel about an event that was supposed to go down. But our intel was wrong, or delayed.

"We got there too late. We arrived just as a bomb went off in a school. Within seconds, the whole place was in flames. There were terrified kids everywhere, running. We helped get as many kids out as we could. I thought maybe everyone had gotten out. And then I saw all these little faces pressed against a second-story window."

She remembered his uneasiness in her classroom. She remembered him telling her to try and get on the first floor. She remembered him saying, "I'm sure you do. Unless there's a fire."

Her heart broke for the look on his face as he remembered this, the helpless agony there. He still wouldn't meet her eyes, as if he carried some unspeakable shame within him, as if somehow this was all his fault. She put her hand across the table and laid it on his wrist.

He looked at it for a moment, as if he understood perfectly what she was offering. Her strength and her compassion.

He shook her hand away.

"We had been ordered to stand down." He was looking at her now. His gaze was aloof. She had liked it better when he was not looking at her, not with this look in his eyes.

"The building was deemed too dangerous for us to go into. Do you understand what an order means when you are in the military?"

She nodded mutely.

"It's not open for discussion. At all. But I couldn't do it. I couldn't stand there and look at those kids and hear their terrified voices coming out the window they had smashed. My mom had just had Henry. I had a little brother and a little sister the same age as those kids."

Isabella had never felt the heartbreak she felt looking into his face. She understood that he was trying to close himself off from her. Connor was a man held in the hell of his own memories. And he was not going to allow anyone to shoulder that burden with him.

"In retrospect, there were other things I

could have done. We could have organized something for them to jump into. We could have stood under the windows and tried to catch them.

"But no," he said softly. "I had to be the cowboy, even though I'm from Corpus Christi. You know, I was a wild kid in my youth. The military managed to tame most of that out of me, but not all of it.

"So, they told us to stand down, and I said those words to my superior that Luigi said to me that day in the hallway, and I think I said them with as much pleasure.

"And I went into that building. If you've never been in a burning building, you have no idea. It's darker than night in there, even though it's the middle of the day. The noise is something that you awake in the night thinking you hear—like the wail of a banshee. It's so hot you can feel your clothes melting.

"But none of that mattered. I was in those doors and up those stairs before I could think it through. What I didn't think through? Once I broke the ranks, they all did. My whole squad, eight men, followed me into that fire."

He was silent for a long, long time.

"Only seven came out," he said. "My best friend was unaccounted for. I went back in one more time. He was trapped under a beam that had fallen. His back was broken. He's in a wheelchair to this day. Because of me. He has burn scars over fifty percent of his body because of me."

"What about the children?" she whispered.

"They made it. Every single one them. To this day, Justin will tell you it was worth it."

"Then maybe you should believe him," she said.

The look Connor gave her was furious. "No. Maybe *you* should believe *me*. I made a decision based totally on emotion. It was unacceptable. When I start coming from that place of emotion, my judgment is clouded."

She saw, instantly, where he was going with this.

"You're saying your judgment is clouded about me," she said.

"Look what happened today. I read that situation all wrong. It's an embarrassment."

"I wasn't embarrassed," she said. "I don't think anything you did could ever embarrass me."

For a moment, it looked as if something in him softened, as if he might lean toward her. But no, he leaned away. He heaved himself up from the table.

She got up and stood in front of him. "Please don't go. Please don't carry this one second longer by yourself."

He stared at her. For a second, once again, he hesitated. She saw so much pain and so much longing in his face. She thought she had him.

But then his face hardened, and he put her out of his way. "Like I need a little chit like you to help me carry my burdens," he snapped. "You'd be squished like a bug underneath them. Like a bug."

And then, casting her one more proud look, he was out the door. She followed him. She could not believe the impotent frustration she felt.

"Connor Benson!"

He swung around and looked at her.

"You are the worst kind of coward," she yelled. "You act as if you are the bravest man alive, but when it comes to matters of your heart? You are a complete coward."

His mouth fell open. Then he folded his arms over his chest and spread his legs apart. A warrior's stance if she had ever seen one. It just made her madder. There was a pot of flowers by her door and, propelled by anger, she picked it up. She hurled it at him. He had to step to one side to avoid being hit. The pot smashed harmlessly beside him. He glared at her, and she glared back, and then he turned and walked away, not once glancing back at her.

She watched him walk down the street, his stride long and confident and powerful, the walk of a warrior, until she could see him no more. And then she closed her kitchen door and leaned against it and wept.

What on earth had gotten into her? She was a demure schoolteacher! She did not scream at people in the streets. Or throw pots at them.

Or slap people. Or wear red dresses. Or green bikinis.

Let's face it. Connor Benson had brought out the worst in her.

Or maybe what he had done was make her lose her hold on control, to find at her center she was not demure at all, but passionate and fiery and alive.

Because despite vibrating with anger at him right now, Isabella had to admit she felt as alive as she had ever felt. Despite the fact he had left her, and she knew he was going to use all his considerable strength never to look back, she still felt on fire with life.

She gathered herself and gathered her

broom and dustpan and went out into the street and cleaned up the mess she had made. And then she brought it into her kitchen and opened the dustbin. But before she dumped the broken pot and flowers and dirt in, she noticed there was something in there that had not been in there before.

She set her filled dustpan on the floor and hauled the trash out from under the sink. She found the pieces of a smashed vase, and the broken stems of wildflowers, and a water-stained note. She carefully pressed open its folds with her fist. She would know that bold handwriting anywhere. She read the note.

Dear Isabella,
Life is a river, with calm places and tur-bulent places. I wonder if you would like to join me on this wild and unpredictable ride? If you are willing, I will pick you up tomorrow evening, after the fete, and we will explore the river.

Instead of signing it with "love," he had drawn a quite adorable heart and then signed his name.

But between the time he had written this note and now, everything had changed. Because of Luigi's father, but not really. That incident had just triggered all of Connor's deepest insecurities.

What a terrible burden to carry through life: to think you were in charge of everything, to want to protect everyone, to not allow yourself any mistakes.

It was a hopeless task, of course, protecting everyone. It was impossible. Connor Benson had set for himself an impossible task, and then he was hard on himself when he failed. What he needed most was not, as she had said, someone to help him carry the burden, though he needed that, too. But what he needed most was someone who could gently tell him when he was being unreasonable, when the goal he had set for himself was too much for one man alone.

What he needed was that safe place, where it was okay to make mistakes, where nobody died or was in danger because you had been wrong.

She knew exactly what Connor Benson needed. He needed her. But how on earth was she going to let him know that?

Over the next few days she tried to find clues to where he had gone, but he had disappeared as if he had never been. He was gone completely, without a trace and without a trail. Her initial fire sputtered out. Isabella sank into the deepest despair of her life.

Where there is deep grief, there was deep love.

It complicated her sense of losing Connor that what she felt now was worse than the loss of her husband. It made the wild tumult inside her worse now that she wondered if she had ever truly loved Giorgio. What had it been, if not love?

She could not eat and she could not sleep. Her whole house was a reminder of Connor—the bed he had slept in, the shower he had saved her from, the kitchen table where they had sat together. She was ashamed with how impatient she was with the children at school. But it seemed she spared Luigi, even though his behavior was worse than ever since his father had come to the fete.

Still, she recognized in the child a great mourning, a great sense of loss. She recognized he was acting out in frustration against helplessness.

And then she was shaken out of her own pity when Luigi disappeared. He didn't arrive at school one morning, and she had received no note from his mother saying he would be absent. The whole town was in an uproar. Had he been kidnapped by his father?

The police were called, and a tense day and night later, Luigi was found asleep under a shrub, a backpack beside him, his face tearstained but his spirit as fierce as ever.

"I am not going to have a life without my papa," he screamed, unrepentant, at his mother in front of the police station.

And this time, she heard him. She wrapped her little boy in her arms and said she understood. That she had been wrong to make him suffer because of her pride. That she would change her stance toward Luigi's father, that she would not stand in the way of them loving one another anymore.

Within days, Isabella could see the changes in Luigi. His father was reintroduced into his life. Luigi was calmer. He was happier. He brought her flowers one day, as if to apologize for all he had put her through.

It was a victory of love, and it made Isabella think.

Was she going to mourn for another six years, then? What if she had been wrong? What if deep love didn't cripple you with grief?

What if deep love made you stronger? What if it made you fight to the death for what you wanted? It was the force that had sent a little boy out looking for his father, knowing what all the adults around him had not known—he *needed* that love.

She needed Connor's love. She wanted to be fully alive. She wanted to feel the way she had felt when she was with him.

She realized there were different kinds of love. There was the kind of love Luigi had for his father. And the kind of love Luigi's mother had for her little boy that had helped her overcome her own bitterness and put what was best for him first.

Yes, there was the kind of love that Isabella had had for Giorgio. Because she had loved Giorgio with gentle compassion did not mean she had loved him less. It meant that she had loved him differently.

And it was all part of her journey to know love completely.

She had to find Connor. She had to convince him not that she was worthy of his love, because she suspected they both knew that. She had to convince him that he was worthy of hers.

She went back to the chapel, sure she could find there some clue to where he would go.

What she found was workmen gone for the day and the fresco, reminding her that beauty was true greatness, and that beauty survived when all else fell away.

She went to the river where she had waded with him. It was warmer now, and there were signs the little boys who had a hung a rope and tire from the tree so they could swing out over the water came more often.

There was no one here now, though, and she took off the cover she had put over the plainest of her bathing suits. She hesitated and then climbed the slippery bank, grabbed the rope with both hands and planted her feet on the tire. She swung way out into the river, where the water was definitely over her head, and even though there was a possibility she could lose everything if she let go of that rope, she let go anyway.

It was exhilarating. It felt wonderful to live life without a safety net. It felt wonderful to take chances. It felt wonderful to be brave.

Life was, indeed, a river, with calm places and turbulent places. It was indeed a wild and unpredictable ride. She had never seen it like that before Connor. She wanted to explore completely the wild and unpredictable ride. She wanted to explore it with him.

It came to her—that incident at the fete. It wasn't just that he felt he had made a mistake. It was the whole thing.

It was the realization he could not stop bad things from happening. He could not stop the tragedy of a marriage not working, children being the victims. He said he had seen that before with his SEAL buddies.

If Luigi's father had had a weapon concealed under his coat, Connor could have stopped that particular tragedy from unfolding, but his work had made him so aware of the next one, waiting. His inability to save his friend had made him way too aware how powerless even the most powerful of men could be.

Isabella suddenly felt drenched in light. She felt as if she was the soldier, not him. She had to go get him. She had to rescue Connor from the lonely world of perfection and protection he had made for himself.

And suddenly, there in that deep pool, enjoying the gift he had given her—a freedom from fear—she knew exactly how to find him.

A day later, her confidence felt more shaky as she dialed the number.

"Itus, Arnold speaking."

The voice was curt and no-nonsense. It

shook her that it was not a name she was expecting.

"I'm looking for someone named Justin."

There was a moment's silence and then wariness. "You've got him."

"My name is Isabella Rossi. I am looking for Connor Benson."

"You and half the civilized world."

"What does that mean?"

Silence. "What did you say your name was?"

"Isabella Rossi."

"I'm going to guess you're from Monte Calanetti, aren't you?"

"That is correct."

"Ah. I should have guessed."

"Guessed?"

"That there was a reason he came back from there grumpier than a bear with a sore bottom."

"I'm that reason?" Grumpier than a bear with a sore bottom?

"I'm asking you. Are you that reason?"

"I think I might be," she said with a sigh. "I need to talk to him. You don't know where he is?"

"He came back, checked in, made my life miserable for a few days, then cleared his schedule and disappeared."

It confirmed exactly what Isabella had suspected. He had not gone back home and dismissed all that had happened to him. He was somewhere nursing his wounds. Alone. Her heart felt as if it was breaking.

Not for herself. For him. For Connor.

"So, you don't know where he is?" Her disappointment felt as sharp as shards of glass.

"I don't right this minute. But if there's one thing I am very, very good at? It's finding people."

"Who don't want to be found?"

"Especially people who don't want to be found. Up until this point, I thought I'd leave him alone. And I will. But if you want to go find him, I'm okay with that. More than okay with that."

In two hours he called her back. Two hours after that, she was on a bus to the city to catch a plane, a ticket for the first flight to Switzerland clutched in her hand.

Connor stared out the window of the mountain cabin. There was really nothing as glorious as the Alps in springtime. He wasn't sure why he had picked a place to hide where he couldn't swim, though.

No, that choice had not been an accident.

His whole life he had chased away strong feelings. It was what his military training had taught him to do. Emotion always got him in trouble. He could swim it off, shake off nearly anything with enough punishing physical activity.

So he couldn't swim, but the mountains all around beckoned. He could hike or climb mountains, or go down to that little public house in the village at the bottom of the mountain and drink himself into oblivion.

But it was the oddest thing that had ever happened to him.

Connor *wanted* to feel this. He wanted to feel the devastating loss of Isabella. He wanted to feel the consequences of his actions. He wanted to wake up in the morning and wonder what the point of life was, to feel his all-encompassing emptiness.

He wanted to remember, in excruciating detail, every second they had spent together. He wanted to remember her joy in the pool, and the way her face had looked when she saw the fresco of the Madonna and child.

He wanted to miss her.

He wanted to feel it all intensely. That was his mission. Miss Isabella. And then be over it, completely, and get back to his life.

Except he had expected the getting-over-it part to be much faster. He was beginning to think the completely part was out of the question. He might have to settle for getting over her a little bit. Enough to function. After all, he'd been in his little cottage in the Alps for a week and if anything, he felt more morose than when he'd begun.

And that did not bode well for whoever knocked on his door. He'd specifically told his landlady he was not to be disturbed under any circumstances.

But of course, she could not control a lost hiker at the door. Or the Swiss equivalent of a Girl Scout selling cookies.

So he swung open the door in a bad temper, ready to be equally unwelcoming to Heidi selling cookies or the lost hiker seeking refuge.

The shock reverberated up his spine when he saw who was there. For a moment, his heart was so filled with gratitude to see the face he had told himself he would never see again that it felt as though he might fall on his knees.

But then he straightened his spine and drew in a deep breath.

He needed to protect her. From himself. From the damaged person he was. From the incomplete person he was. She deserved so much better.

"Isabella." He heard the coolness in his voice and saw the purpose in her posture falter just a bit.

"Connor."

Again, his knees felt weak at the way she said his name. It came off her lips like a blessing, as if she saw all of him and accepted that completely.

"Why are you here?" he asked harshly.

"I'm here to rescue you. I tried to send a Saint Bernard with a cask of whiskey around his neck, but apparently they don't do that anymore."

He did not want to be charmed by her!

"You look horrible," she said softly.

He already knew that! He had looked at his own reflection this morning in the mirror, made the decision not to shave, again. His hair was uncombed, his clothes were rumpled—he looked like a wild man, as if he was holed up in a cave, not in a perfectly civilized cabin.

"Can I come in?"

"There's no point."

She ignored him and slipped under his arm into the cottage.

"Hey!"

"Wow," she said, looking around.

He turned and saw the place through her eyes. It was an absolute shambles. Clothes on the floor, dirty dishes on every surface. There was a bag of groceries by the small kitchen that he had not even bothered to unpack. A trail of cookie crumbs went across the floor and disappeared under a pair of socks.

It was as if it was the first time he'd really noticed it in days. Who had he become? He was a fastidiously neat person.

Undeterred by how the mess spoke to his character, Isabella went over, frowned at the couch and then delicately moved two newspapers and an empty container of chocolate fudge ice cream out of her way. She sat down as if she planned to stay.

"What do you want?" he asked, folding his arms over his chest. He tapped his foot and glanced at his watch. She looked so unperturbed by his show of impatience that he felt almost panicky. He was going to have to be mean to her.

To Isabella? That was impossible.

But it was for her own good. He took a deep breath, soldiered himself. This was what he did. He did hard things. He did impossible things.

"Look, you've traveled a long way for nothing," he said. "If you're going to tell me you can't live without me, forget it. I'm not moved by emotion."

"Hmm," she said, again unperturbed.

He frowned at her.

"I think I came to tell you that you can't live without me," she decided. He contemplated the awful truth of that, and he contemplated the fact she had seen it so clearly. This was not about her. Not in any way. It was about him.

"Well, I can. Live without you. And I will."

"Quit being so damned strong," she said softly. "You've had to be so strong your whole life, Connor. You started working when you were eleven years old to help look after your mom."

"That's hitting below the belt," he said, "bringing my mom into it."

"What is this, below the belt?"

"You're an adult woman—I think you can figure out where men don't like to get hit."

She nodded, mulling that over, but then kept on talking as if he hadn't warned her. "So you've always felt protective of your poor mother, who had you very young and was abandoned by the people who should have supported her. Is it any surprise you were drawn to a profession where you protect people, where you try and fix things? Everything?"

"Look, Little Red Riding Hood, just skip on home. You're playing with the Big Bad Wolf here, and that story does not end well, if you recall."

She cocked her head at him. She didn't look even slightly intimidated. He considered the possibility he was losing his touch.

"You have carried the weight of the whole world for way, way too long," she decided softly.

"Says you."

She sighed as if he was no more irritating to her than Luigi Caravetti yelling swearwords. "I thought we should have a discussion. About the river of life."

He groaned. "Have you no pride? Picking through the garbage?"

"None at all," she said. "Not when it comes to you. It's your turn, Connor."

"My turn?" he said warily.

"Your turn to be rescued."

"You've already said that. Saint Bernards on strike, you have come in their place, without the cask."

"I brought something better than the cask."

He went very still. He knew what she had brought. He could see what she had brought shining from her eyes. He could see it shining from the very fiber of her being.

He could fight anything. That was what he had been trained to do. To fight. And he was so good at it.

But he was not sure that he could fight this. *Don't ask her*, he begged himself, *don't ask her what she brought. You aren't strong enough, Connor, you aren't.*

"What did you bring?" His voice was a rasp.

"You know," she said softly. "You already know what I brought."

Even before she said the words, he could feel his every defense beginning to crumble, like a dam made out of mud and sticks giving way after holding everything in for way too long, so long that its strength had already been compromised.

"I brought love," she said. "I brought my love to rescue you."

"No, please. Isabella, don't do this."

She was up off that sofa in a heartbeat. She navigated the mess on his floor and stood in front of him. She shined with a fierce light.

So, love could be this, too. Not just gentle

and sweet and quiet and compliant. But this: as strong as steel forged in a fire.

She put her hands on both sides of his face and forced him to look her in the eyes, look into those great green-and-gold pools of strength and compassion.

"You be whoever you need to be," she said softly. "You be a warrior going to do battle. You be the man who rushes into burning buildings. You be that man who seeks out danger like a heat-seeking missile seeks warmth. You be the man who sees the potential for bad things on a beautiful spring afternoon in the village square. You be the man who would lay down his life to protect a bride on her wedding day. You be those things."

Her words were like the final drops of water adding pressure to the already compromised structure of the dam. Her words broke Connor wide-open. He felt as if he had waited all his life for this one moment, for these words of acceptance, these words of someone seeing him exactly as he was and moving toward him anyway.

She continued to drop words, like healing raindrops, into the brokenness inside him.

"And then you come back to me," she said, and her voice was a promise that he could feel himself moving toward, that every ounce of his strength could not have stopped him from moving toward.

"And you show me all the bruised places," Isabella said, her voice fierce and true, "and the brokenness of your heart. You show me, and me alone, what it has cost you to be these things. And you let me place poultices on your bruises, and you let me knit my love around your wounds.

"Connor, I will be the place where you lay down your sword. I will be the place where you see that beauty wins. I will be the home that shows you that love survives all things, and makes all things possible."

He was staring at her. His heart was pounding as if he had run a race, and he could see the finish line. She, Isabella Rossi, was the finish line, and he reached out for her.

He reached out and scraped his hand down her cheek. He realized she was crying, and he was pretty sure she did not know that herself.

"You look just like her right now," he said, his voice soft.

"Who? Who do I look like?"

He gazed at her, feeling as if he could never get enough. When he spoke, his voice was hoarse with emotion. "The Madonna in the fresco. You look just like her."

He stared at her, not able to look away, held by the light that had infused her face, aware that he was in the presence of the purest and most powerful thing in the world.

Rarely, like in the fresco, someone captured the essence of this power, the heart of it, the spirit of it. An unknown Renaissance artist had followed inspiration, obeyed it and been allowed to capture it.

It was love.

It was all that it was to be human at its highest and its best. It was what Connor had fought his whole life for, without ever being able to give it a name.

He realized he was like the man in Greek mythology, just as Isabella had said, a long time ago. He *was* like Itus. He was being offered the opportunity to walk among gods. For that was what it was for a man to know love. It was to walk in glory. It was to experience things beyond what a mortal man had a right to expect.

He did not deserve this. He knew that. And he also knew that it didn't matter. That he was not strong enough to refuse what was being offered to him.

Connor Benson did what he had never done, not in his whole life. Even when he was a child, he had stood strong, he had been ready to fight for what he felt was right. But now, standing here before Isabella, drenched in the light, he bowed before her, and before the presence of a force greater than himself.

He laid down his weapons. He laid his head on her shoulder. He surrendered. He ate the food that was offered to him.

He felt Isabella's hand, cool and strong, on the back of his neck. He felt her tears anoint him. And he drew her into the warmth of himself and held her in a way that reflected the truths he had just learned.

He held Isabella as if he would never let her go.

He was a man who had crossed deserts, navigated jungles, climbed mountains. He was a man who had fought to give others something that he had not named. But now that he was there, in the circle of its light, he recognized the name of it.

Home.

Connor Benson was home.

* * * * *

LARGER-PRINT BOOKS!
GET 2 FREE LARGER-PRINT NOVELS PLUS
2 FREE GIFTS!

◊ HARLEQUIN®

Romance

From the Heart, For the Heart

"I'm here about the position you advertised for a housekeeper."

His eyebrows shot up. His gaze swept her. "Oh," he said, "that."

"Yes, that."

He gave her another long look, apparently contemplating her suitability for the position. She tried for her most housekeeperly expression.

"Especially nope to that," he said firmly.

When the door began to whisper shut again, it was pure desperation that made Angie put one foot in to stop it.

The man—good God, was he Heathcliff from *Wuthering Heights*—glanced down at her foot with astonished irritation. And then he gave her a look so icily reserved it should have made her withdraw her foot and touch her forelock immediately. But it did not. Angie held her ground.

She refused to retreat. She couldn't!

After a moment, he sighed again, and again she felt the sensuous heat of his breath whisper across her cheek.

Then he opened the door wide and leaned the breadth of one of those amazing shoulders against the jamb, the seeming casualness of the stance not fooling her. Every fiber of his being was practically vibrating with displeasure. He folded his arms over the immenseness of his chest, and tilted his head at her, waiting for an explanation for her audacity.

Really, all that icy remoteness should not have made him more attractive. But the impatient frown tugging at the edges of those too-stern lips made her think renegade thoughts of what was beyond the ice, and what it would be like to find out.

These, Angie reminded herself sternly, were crazy thoughts. This man was making her think crazy thoughts. She was a woman who had suffered so completely at the hands of love.

With that kind of track record, it made her thoroughly annoyed with herself for even noticing what the master of the Stone House looked like. And what his voice sounded like. And what he smelled like. And what his breath had felt like grazing the tenderness of her cheek.

If she had a choice, she would have cut and run. But she was desperate. She had absolutely no choice.

With her foot against the door he was too polite to slam, she said, determined, "I need this job."

Don't miss
HOUSEKEEPER UNDER THE MISTLETOE
by Cara Colter, available November 2015 wherever
Harlequin® Romance books and ebooks are sold.

www.Harlequin.com

HREXP1015